The Six of Salem
The Magic Awak
Kristin Bapst

Prologue – Salem 1692

She knew they'd be coming soon. She handed Lia the baby, wrapped in a blanket, and she stuffed an item in her satchel.

"Take care of her." she pleaded.

"I will." Lia promised.

"And make sure the bloodline and the power survives."

"You won't be forgotten." Lia swore.

"Go – now!" she urged.

Lia closed the door of her shack in silence and headed for the woods, where their secret place was. She knew Luke would accept the child as their own. They would teach her from the book. They would instill a code of honor.

Back at the colony, people pounded on the door and torches glowed through the windows.

As the door was kicked in, she screamed.

Chapter One

Rayna stretched the length of her bed, yawning. She threw off the purple and green hand-sewn quilt, and started to get up.

Rayna got up and went into the bathroom, scrubbing her face with Dove soap. She rinsed and brushed her teeth and jumped in the shower. Rayna closed her eyes as the cool water cascaded over her body. She soaped up with pumpkin spice scented shower gel and washed her hair with shampoo for curly hair.

Rayna dried off with a plush towel and did her makeup. As she stood in her bedroom, she looked in her full length mirror at her body. She had full hips, generous breasts, toned calves, thick thighs, and a plump back end – why was she single for three years?

Then she slipped into a long-sleeve black top with exposed shoulders and forearms and a pair of jeggings. On her feet, were black Converse sneakers. She put her rune stone bracelet on that her aunt gave her. She said it was to protect her, though she couldn't understand why'd she would need it.

Rayna walked through the brick streets Salem. The sun shone through the fiery color of the trees. Rayna saw an occult shop and paused. There was a love spell book on display. She bit her lip. Rayna took a few steps forward, paused, then hurried off to the local cafe.

She walked a block to the cafe and got a cinnamon scone & pumpkin spice latte. It was her daily routine.

Rayna walked down the block with her breakfast in hand. Her dark brown curls were ruffled by the slight wind. Her blue eyes gleamed in the sunlight. Her caramel toned skin glistened with sweat. It was late September – still hot enough for sweat to bead Rayna's forehead and make her clothes feel like they were damp.

She entered *Midnight Tomes*, the bookstore she co-owned with her aunt. It smelled of sage and lavender. The shelves, cabinets, and counter were oak, with a glass case containing several witchcraft items too expensive to be out in the open, including cauldrons, expensive gemstones, and daggers. The cabinets contained herbs, smudging materials, oils, and various scented waters. There was also a display of incense out on the floor.

Rayna went behind the counter, putting her coffee down after taking a sip and called out.

"Nakiyah!"

A dark-skinned slim woman with braids throughout her hair walked out from the stacks.

"I knew you'd be late."

"You wouldn't fire your own niece, would you?" Rayna asked with a smile.

"You've got me there." Nakiyah replied, with a smirk.

"Can you go through the stacks and find some books? I have someone who placed an order online. The payment is taken care of, but I need you to package them up for me." Nakiyah requested, handing her a list.

"Sure." Rayna agreed, taking a gulp of her coffee as she went to the shelves.

'Hm. Book of Shadows. Wicca: The Solitary Practitioner. Teen Witch.'

Rayna went through the stacks and piled the three books up. She brought them to the front, wrapped them in silver sparkle paper, and placed them in a brown bag with their symbol on the front – a witch in front of a crescent moon. Cliché, but it worked.

"Can you take care of the bills?" Nakiyah asked.

Rayna took her coffee with her into the back room. The financials were laid out for her, complete with calculator, red pen, and pencil. Their profits came in ample streams – they were never late with any bills, and they donated some of their earnings to charities.

As Rayna tapped away at the calculator and scribbled in numbers, she heard raised voices.

Shouting and cursing in a foreign language.

'What the hell is going on?'

The door slammed shut. Rayna tried to go back to the financials, but she was couldn't focus.

Who would her aunt start an argument with?

She made a note in her head to ask her later

* * *

Salem – 1692

Samuel waited in the center of the woods, pacing. He had taken one of his cows and slaughtered it, burning it on a bonfire, and making the sign with its blood.

They would be coming. He knew it.

The wind suddenly picked up and leaves turned into a small funnel.

A spark of fire and he appeared.

He was wearing a black robe with a hood, his eyes blood red.

"So...you've decided." he growled, smiling with a smile of teeth like knives.

"I want immortality in return. And I want that devilish whore to die!" Samuel exclaimed.

"Oh, her?" the demon asked with sarcasm.

"Don't you dare mock me!" Samuel snapped.

"CONSIDER WHO YOU ARE TALKING TO!" the man roared.

Samuel fell back on the ground, trembling.

"I will give you what you ask. But you will repay."

"Isn't the sacrifice enough?" Samuel murmured.

"No. You can accuse whoever you want. They will be found guilty, they will be gone – and we will take their souls. And since we're getting all of theirs..." he paused, "...will only take half of yours."

"Half my soul?" he asked incredulously.

"You thought a demon from the bowels of Hell would leave without taking part of you?" he asked, "You will only have half your soul left – and so will anyone you make a compact with. You will get your immortality. And the souls will be mine." he growled.

Samuel took a deep breath.

He kneeled before the man, hanging his head.

"Take it." he offered with humbleness, "Just give me what I ask."

The man grinned again.

He reached into the man's throat and removed part of a white wisp that wriggled in his grasp.

"Do not fight me," he warned, "I will win."

Samuel held his arms out and arched his back, shaking as half of him was taken.

The demon swallowed it, letting out a satisfied breath. Blood dripped from the corner of his mouth.

"They will all suffer. And you will have me over your head for all eternity," he laughed, "But you know that. After all..." he trailed off, "You can see the wicked, can't you?" he finished with the same smile.

Samuel noticed he felt...empty. No tears. No love. No pity. They would suffer.

She would die. He just had to find her descendants when the time was right. He would bide his time before he started the war he wanted.

"This is what you wanted." the demon husked, placing a clawed hand on his head.

He bowed his head to the ground and a fire came up. It surrounded him, smoke rising. When they both dissipated, he was gone.

"The time has come. Pay your dues." a deep voice roared.

Samuel ran to the village. Many people would die. But he found he didn't care.

Chapter Two

Rayna exited the back room with the financials book, taking the last sip of her coffee and discarding the cup in the waste basket. She saw the bag of books was gone.

"Nakiyah?" she called, wandering the stacks.

She found her browsing the books.

"What are you looking for?" she asked.

"Oh, a customer called...they wanted a specific book that I'm trying to find."

"What's the title? Maybe I can help you." Rayna offered.

The door jingled.

"Can you go to the front?" Nakiyah asked.

Rayna walked to the register to find a woman in a black shawl with silver stars and moons all over it with a black dress underneath.

"I came here for white sage and heart chakra incense." the customer requested.

Rayna turned to the cabinet behind her and picked out a bunch of white sage and a packet of heart chakra incense.

"Do you need a smudge bowl?" Rayna asked.

"I have one, thanks." the woman replied smiling.

Rayna rang her up, took the payment, and the customer left in silence.

She noticed a book of love spells on display in the window. She grabbed it, put money in the register, and stuffed it in her messenger bag before her aunt could see.

Nakiyah came to the front with the book, quickly wrapped it up in silver paper, and stuck it in a bag.

"Do you want me to take care of that transaction?" Rayna asked.

"No, thank you Rayna, but I can do it. Why don't you put up the decorations for Halloween?" she asked.

A man passed by the window, and his eyes met with Rayna's. She couldn't tear herself away. His eyes were a deep ocean blue that sent chills through her.

"Rayna!" Nakiyah called.

Rayna turned and saw Nakiyah give the man slitted eyes and pursed lips. He sped past the store, Rayna disappointed he disappeared.

"Nakiyah...is that the man you were shouting at? What was going on?" Rayna asked with caution.

"It was just a disgruntled customer. He said the corners of the books were bent, and that they were dusty." Nakiyah replied, staring into the pages of the financials.

"It couldn't have been that simple if -"

"I took care of it. It's done." Nakiyah paused, "There are tourists exiting a bus. I must go beckon them in."

Nakiyah went outside with her pearly smile and rattled off bestselling titles and their popular herbs. A few people came in to browse. Her aunt stood behind the register and waved Rayna off.

Rayna sighed. She went into the storage room to get out their Samhain decorations.

Something was up.

She just didn't know what.

* * *

That night, Rayna put on a kettle and put a lavender stress relief tea bag in her mug.

For dinner, Rayna made herself a salad with romaine, cucumber, and tomato – drizzling on Italian dressing. Once the water boiled she brought the meal and her tea into the living space. She turned on the TV and put on The Voice.

As Rayna listened to Blake and Adam insult each other, watched Jennifer throw her shoe, and saw Gwen lean over and kiss Blake's cheek, she found herself laughing and smiling.

Rayna forgot about today.

However, once it was over, she turned off the TV and sat up in her bed, exhausted. She stared at the print of a Monet painting on the wall and wished her life was different.

Morning clean-up and dressing – scone and coffee – work – then a salad with a cup of tea. Sure, Rayna had her aunt, but she wanted more.

She had a few boyfriends, but they all ghosted her and moved on.

Rayna missed having love in her life.

Someone to confide her secrets in.

Someone who understood her.

She curled under her sheets, clutching her bear stuffed animal from childhood to her heart.

* * *

Salem – 1692

He laid in the scratchy bed next to her. He looked deep into her eyes and stroked her face. He had salt and pepper hair and blue eyes. He kissed her with tenderness and wrapped his arms around her.

"You have bewitched me." he whispered.

"My herbs worked then." she said, with a smile, brushing back her braids.

"Was it that tea you gave me? What was it – rosemary?"

"That's not why we are here together." she crooned, running her hand through his hair.

He kissed her passionately and lowered his head to her breast, taking it in his mouth. She arched her back and rubbed her knee against his hardness. He moaned.

"Enough," she gasped, "He will be home soon. Working the fields won't last forever."

She got up and slipped her dress and apron back on.

"If only we could have a homestead together..." she trailed off, "I could make you delicious food, tend to your children, make a good home. I'm tired of hiding what we have – sneaking around in the evening hours."

He came up behind her, dressed, and wrapped his arms around her.

"So...what..I preach sermons about damnation, leave my wife, and marry a witch? We would both be drowned." he argued.

She stiffened. He felt it.

"I'm just saying it would never work – our relationship would be punished. I don't want to think of what could happen to you. It's...best we end it. I've been married and respected by Salem for a long time." He explained, releasing her.

A tear trailed down her cheek.

"You may leave. And never come back." She said with steel in her voice.

"That's it?" he asked incredulously.

"I am banishing you." she said, "I will cook your meals, tend to your children, tend to your wife, keep house. But we are over."

His face reddened.

How dare that woman reject him!

He slammed the door behind him and walked the dirt path to his house. His daughters were probably making dinner – his wife was with her knitting group.

As he walked in the house, he came upon Elizabeth convulsing on the wooden living room floor, her eyes rolling back in her head.

"My dearest! What happened to you?" he asked.

She was unable to answer, choking on her tongue. He sat her up, trying to get her to breathe, but then she fell in his arms.

Dead.

A dark look came over his face.

No one hurt his daughters.

Rayna shot straight up in her bed, stiff. She was confused. Why would she have a vision of herself with that man? That was all she remembered – the feel of his arms around her, his lips, his hardness against her pelvis, his soft whispers.

It felt nice.

But she didn't remember his face.

'Must be my imagination. Too many hours spent in that bookshop.'

She clutched her pillow and drifted off into a dreamless sleep.

Chapter Three

Rayna took a deep breath of the fresh air. It was her day off – tourists never came on Sundays.

Probably superstition. She knew some people who felt if they visited shops there on a Sunday, lightning would come down and strike them. She laughed to herself.

Rayna reached into her messenger bag and opened the book she bought.

"Attract Your Soul Mate" the page read.

She scanned the list of items and walked with haste to *Midnight Tomes*.

Rayna unlocked the door and went behind the counter. She put the money in the register and stuffed them in her backpack.

She locked the door and walked down the street to a flower vendor. She bought a few pink and red roses and made sure she put them down in the bag with gentleness.

Afterwards, Rayna walked two blocks to the cafe. She ordered a blueberry scone and a pumpkin spice latte. The barista handed her the latte. As the cashier handed her the scone in a bakery bag, she froze.

"These blueberries are from our farm." the man whispered, feeding them one by one into her mouth.

She let her tongue run over his fingers as she ate them, her hand grasping his.

"So sweet." she murmured.

"Love goes into these." he insisted.

"Love is magic in and of itself." she replied.

He kissed her deeply, his hand cupping her face as she stroked his chest.

Rayna felt the latte slip from her hand, and that's when she awoke again. But before it could hit the floor, she saw a hand grab it and lift it up to her.

"Is this yours?" the voice asked.

Rayna looked at the person and saw a man. He had long brown hair and scruff forming into a goatee. His eyes were deep blue, and he had a gentle smile. She smelled some kind of cologne, and his voice was firm yet gentle and soft.

"Yes..." Rayna stammered.

"Are you okay?" he asked, "You seemed out of it."

"Yeah, I'm fine. I just...zoned out for a minute."

"Look, why don't you sit with me and my daughter – so you don't fall over again?" he offered.

"Okay." Rayna agreed, shakily.

He took her hand and began to lead her to the table. His teenage daughter was sitting there with a bagel and a cup of something hot.

"This is Rose." he said, looking at his daughter, "I'm sorry what's your name?" he asked her.

"Rayna."

"Rose, can you be polite and say hi to Rayna?"

"Hi," she mumbled, tapping away on her smartphone.

"She's usually not a millenial." he explained.

"So I've never seen you around." Rayna mentioned.

"Oh we just moved here a few weeks ago."

"What do you do?" he asked.

"I run the occult bookstore in town. It's called *Midnight Tomes*." she replied.

"I've heard of it.." he trailed off.

"What about you?" she asked.

"Oh, I'm involved with a natural foods store that just moved here. I basically choose the inventory."

"So do you eat what you sell?" she asked.

"Yes, very much so." he said, grinning.

"You should meet my aunt."

"Yeah...maybe..." he paused.

"Well I think I've gotten my head straight now," Rayna brushed off, not wanting to seem too interested, "I'll see you around town."

She exited the bakery and headed down the street.

"Do you think it'll be different this time?" Rose asked.

"I hope so." her father said.

"Never is." Rose mumbled, continuing to tap away on her phone.

As he watched Rayna walk away, he felt his heart skip a beat.

But he couldn't go back to the bookstore.

* * *

Salem – 1692

Lia entered the shack with the baby and her satchel. Luke hurried over to her.

"This is her?" he asked.

"Yes, this is Ivy."

"Why Ivy?" he asked.

"It's the plant she insisted protected her house," she murmured, shedding a tear.

"I know." he said, grabbing her shoulders, "But you have to be strong for her. And for Ivy. She entrusted us with her child."

She handed him the baby, and she reached into her satchel, bringing out a leather-bound book.

"Is this..." he trailed off.

"Yes," she admitted, "She said to keep it in the bloodline."

"Where do we hide it in the meantime?" he asked.

She kneeled on the wooden floor and pried up a floorboard. She stuck the book in her satchel underneath it and replaced the floorboard, pounding the nails back in with a small hammer.

"Someone will hear!" he insisted.

"No one will find us – they never have. And when they see the place, they assume it's an abandoned, burned out house," she said, "Lucky thing we never rebuilt the place. The shabby look does well for us."

He looked deep into Ivy's green eyes.

"You're ours now," he coddled, "But you will never forget where you came from. We will teach you your mother's ways."

He kissed her forehead and she giggled.

Lia smiled. They were safe.

But her brow furrowed when she thought about her friend.

What would they do to her?

Chapter Four

Rayna tore off the rose petals in bunches, floated them on the surface of the hot water, and poured some of the rose water into the bath. The pink and red votive candles were on the edge of the sink where she could see them. She carved hearts into them and anointed them with rosemary essential oil. She stripped off her clothes and sunk her body into the water. She hugged her knees and let some tears slip out.

Her last relationship ended when her boyfriend met her aunt. His name was Shawn, and he was antsy all through dinner and wouldn't look her in the eye. He came to dinner wearing a God Forbid t-shirt, baggy black jeans, and combat boots – while Rayna wore a fitted emerald dress and heels. After dessert, he made an excuse about going to work early in the morning and hustled out the door. Rayna knew he wasn't working. When she asked her aunt why he did that, Nakiyah shrugged.

Rayna wiped away her tears and looked into the flames of the candles.

She froze.

"I'm off to work." *a light skinned man said, kissing her.*

"See you for dinner, honey." she said, watching him go out the door.

When he left, she lit a homemade beeswax candle. She went outside and picked some red roses and brought them in the house. She sprinkled them around the base of the candle. Then she murmured an incantation, holding her hands over the candle.

A knock came at the door an hour later.

She opened it to see her owner standing there.

"Ma'am," he greeted, tipping his hat, "I wonder if I could come in for a cup of tea."

They locked eyes. A fire burned in them both.

"I have rosemary tea," she said, taking a kettle of water off the stove and pouring it into two mugs.

He sipped the tea, as did the woman, and they gazed into each other's eyes. He pulled at his collar.

"I'm getting rather warm – maybe I should've brought a cold drink." he chuckled.

"That's what this tea is meant to do." she whispered, her eyes glistening amber.

"Warm me up? To you?" he asked, licking his lips.

"Maybe. I've heard about the sermons you preach. I heard that you shout about sin and salvation. In my religion...we believe in love. There is no sin – simply do unto others as you would have them do unto you – whatever you do comes back to you times three."

"Sounds...interesting.." he trailed off, walking towards her.

He unwrapped the fabric around her head and released her braided hair. He entwined his fingers in them and pulled her mouth to his, kissing her with passion, his tongue stroking her mouth. She moaned and clutched at him, her knees weak.

He pulled away and unbuttoned the top of her blouse, pulling the cloth away and kissing her shoulder and collarbone. She took him by the neck and brought his head up, gazing into his eyes.

"So mote it be." she whispered.

"What does that mean?" he asked.

"Nothing." she lied.

"Your skin..." he trailed off, kissing her bare arms, "It's so soft."

"I know something else that's soft." she said, smiling.

He ripped at her dress and backed her onto the bed.

"My beloved." she praised, unbuttoning his shirt and taking it off, then starting on his pants.

He entered her and she moaned. It was fast and rough, both of them like ships on a stormy sea.. When she screamed, it felt like it shook the heavens. He cried out and thrust one last time and collapsed, heaving breath.

As she gasped for air, she felt the baby move inside her.

If he knew she was carrying John's baby, it wouldn't have mattered.

She enchanted him.

And he was hers.

Rayna awoke as her head was slipping under the water. She could've drowned. She pulled herself up and reached between her legs, enjoying the slippery friction. She shouted, crying out a name she didn't know. Samuel.

* * *

On Sunday, Rayna sat in the local pub, eating a burger and drinking a pint of Guinness. She was browsing a book on mysticism and dreams she took from the store, leaving payment in the register. What she found wasn't helpful so far – it was mostly a dream dictionary – but she came across one part that caught her attention.

"A trance often comes over those who have flashbacks that appear as dreams. They often show either the future or the past. When the person wakes up, few details are remembered, except for sensations or emotions."

She wondered if she was going to meet someone with that name.

As Rayna chewed a french fry, the door jingled and she felt a presence by her side.

"So we meet again." the deep voice greeted.

"If we're going to keep running into each other, I should at least know your name." Rayna said, smirking.

"Matthew." he answered, trailing off, "Do you smell roses?" he asked.

"I didn't notice, no." she lied.

"Mind if I join you?" he asked.

"Sure, I guess." she replied.

"What'll it be sir?" the server asked.

"I'll have a porterhouse steak with fried potatoes." he ordered.

"Hm. Typical man." she mused.

"I fit no stereotype." he argued.

"Sure, Mr. Steak and Potatoes." she joked.

"Get to know me, and you'll see." he replied.

The flame of the candle on the table started to dance.

Her heart started to beat a little faster.

The candle flame stilled.

"Well, tell me this. Who is your favorite band?" he asked.

"Disturbed." she replied.

"Ooh, a metalhead."

"Kind of," she admitted, "Though their cover of 'The Sound of Silence' was amazing."

"Yes, it was." he agreed, smiling.

"So tell me about yourself, since you want me to know you." she asked.

"Well...I came from a suburban town. We moved around from place to place because I kept changing jobs. And it worked out because, at the last place we lived, my daughter was bullied. I got this job at the same time. Synchronicity. The teens at this school are much more accepting." he explained.

"Look where they live." Rayna added.

He nodded in agreement, cutting off a piece of steak and taking a small wedge of potato.

"So why are you single?" Rayna asked.

"My wife died a few years ago..." Matthew trailed off.

"What happened?" she asked.

"Freak accident. Sudden." he brushed off.

"Well I hope you find happiness."

"I think I will here." Matthew agreed.

"What do you do on days off?" Rayna asked.

"I tend to binge on movies and television series – relax with a cup of coffee and a chocolate croissant from where I work." Matthew answered.

"What ones do you binge? I have been following The Bold Type and I watch pro wrestling."

"Weird combination – millenials who work at a Cosmo-type magazine and people who beat each other up." Matthew chuckled.

"Well...they talk about real women's issues. And wrestling has characters I relate to – like Nikki Cross. She totally embodies my fun, wild side."

"Good to know," Matthew said, smiling, "Me, I like Legends of Tomorrow, Jessica Jones, Luke Cage."

"Oh, so you're a superhero?" Rayna asked with a smirk.

"Yup. I'm here to save the day." Matthew said, flexing his biceps.

"So," Matthew began, "Read anything good lately?"

"No," Rayna said, slipping the book into her bag, "The last book I read was 'Horns' by Joe Hill. Then I found a used copy of the movie. Amazing stuff."

"I'll have to check those out." he admitted, "I'm more of a Stephen King fan. I loved 'The Shining', 'Duma Key', and 'Bag of Bones'."

"I can loan the 'Horns' book and DVD to you. Actually, my apartment isn't far from here. I could run over there, grab them, and bring them back."

"Why don't I walk you?" Matthew offered.

"I may be getting to know you, but no."

"You've been burned?" he asked, tipping her head up.

"More times than I care to look back on," Rayna paused, "Look, let me run over to my place. I'll be right back." she said, trotting out the door.

As the hostess poked at the fire, a flame rose and she stepped back with a jostle.

The door jingled twenty minutes later and she jogged back in. Rayna handed him the book and DVD.

"I gotta go, but enjoy them. And just give them back next time you see me." she said.

He got up – chivalry wasn't dead – and he looked into her eyes.

The fire in the hearth started sparking wildly.

Rayna shook his hand, and the sparks died down.

As she walked out the door, he stared.

Maybe this time would be different.

Nakiyah stood in the inventory room, checking off packing slips.

She couldn't get that man out of her mind.

She stopped what she was doing and focused her clairvoyance. She closed her eyes and lost herself in the whirls of time.

"We could go pumpkin picking." he suggested.

"For our small house?" she replied, smiling.

"Doesn't mean we can't decorate for the equinox."

"Look!" she said, pointing, "Free apple cider!"

"Whatever you want, my dear." he said.

They kissed and a flame caught on a piece of hay.

"No!" Nakiyah shouted, exiting her vision, clutching her head.

The door jingled.

She composed herself and went out to the front of the store. She saw Rayna entering, sipping a cup of coffee, and holding a book, her eyes scanning the pages.

"Why are you reading a dream book?" Nakiyah asked, trembling inside.

"No reason," Rayna lied, "I just want to see what all these tourists are so crazy about."

"Well...people go nuts for the kitsch. Dream books aren't a big seller..." she trailed off.

"I was just curious." Rayna replied.

Rayna placed her coffee on the counter and turned around the sign to 'Open'. She stepped behind the register and toyed with the artificial fall flowers in the vase.

"I met someone," she mentioned, "That guy you argued with."

"Oh, you did?" Nakiyah asked, her mind spinning.

"Yeah. He seems like a nice guy. It'd be nice to have someone..."

"Oh, but sweetie, he has a teenage daughter. And he just moved here. He's probably just enthralled with the tourism, and won't stay long. Don't tie yourself down to a wanderer." Nakiyah tried to convince Rayna, her voice shaking.

"True, he could be a drifter. But he does seem kind."

"There's more to people than you can really see sometimes."

"And you can?" Rayna asked, an eyebrow raised.

"No, of course not..." Nakiyah excused, fixing her braids, "I just want you to be careful. If you want to meet someone, why don't you try the singles scene?"

"Maybe." Rayna agreed.

Just then, a customer came in.

"You can help them, honey. I'm stuck doing inventory."

"Not a problem, Nakiyah." Rayna replied.

As Rayna took out some herbs for the customer and rang up a book called Moon & Solstice Rituals, she remembered a black spiderweb design dress she had in her closet.

She smiled.

Chapter Five

Rayna looked at herself in the mirror. Stiletto heel black boots, the black dress, and some rhinestone jewelry. She slipped on a light black cardigan and headed out, locking her door and walking a few blocks to the bar.

As she entered she marveled at the place. Mahogany floors and tables, a marble topped bar, LED lighting, and a glowing wall of alcohol, with several taps up front.

Rayna sat at the bar and ordered a glass of sangria. She sipped it, but it went down quick. She found herself ordering glass after glass, but not feeling the effects. She wondered why.

A man approached her in a navy button down suit and black slacks. He had a silver chain around his neck, golden brown slicked back hair, and green eyes.

"Hey, gorgeous." he said, sliding his martini over.

"Hi." Rayna muttered, sipping her sangria.

"I'm Richard. I work in real estate."

"What kind of real estate?" she asked, looking at him closely.

"Condos and penthouses. I work for a major firm."

"I see..." Rayna trailed off.

"Would you like to come see my penthouse? It has a king size bed, black-out drapes, and I read a book on bondage & dominance. So I know what women want." he said putting a hand on her lower back.

Rayna removed his hand.

"That sounds like something a douchebag would say. Do the women in here a favor and leave." she spat.

"Bitch." he muttered, taking his drink to the end of the bar and talking up a skinny blonde.

As Rayna ordered a ginger ale with a shot of Fireball, her sangria finished, another man approached her.

"So are you into rock music?" the guy asked.

He had spiked black hair, a soul strip, and dark eyes lined with black eye liner. He had a nose ring and several earrings.

"Yeah." Rayna said, sipping her spiked ginger ale.

"Right on, girl. We do Whitensake, Warrant, Journey, and Bon Jovi covers. We tried to make Springsteen into 80's hair metal, but it didn't work."

"Don't go to New Jersey. They'd swarm you, and you wouldn't escape alive."

"Nah. We are survivors."

"Not in Jersey." Rayna muttered.

"By the way, I'm Jerry. Can I buy you a drink? Or get you tickets to one of our shows? I can give you a tour of the backstage, including our dressing room." he murmured, kissing her neck.

She pushed him hard and he fell over a barstool.

"Don't you dare do that! Get the fuck out of here! I'm not a groupie!" she yelled, her eyes glowing blue.

He stumbled out of the bar, his eyes widened. As she calmed down and took a gulp of her drink, she shook her head.

Why did I think this was a good idea? Oh right, Nakiyah. She will pay for this.

A man sat next to her in a black and white pinstripe suit, salt and pepper hair, and a garnet ring on his finger. He flashed her a closed mouth smile.

He stared at her.

"Can I help you?" Rayna asked, raising an eyebrow.

"No," he began, "There's something familiar about you."

"Are you from around here?"

"I'm from everywhere – I travel around a lot for my corporate job." he explained.

"Well, nice to meet you." Rayna said, going back to her drink.

"Can I order you another one?" he asked.

"No, thank you. I think I'm done for the night."

She tried to get up and he took her wrist and sat her back down.

"Come on, I don't bite." he crooned, eyeing her, "You remind me of someone I used to know."

"You're not my type, and I don't date guys looking for their ex's. Now let me go, I'm leaving."

"Like hell you are," he growled, gripping her wrist tight, "No one says NO to me. Especially not you."

Rayna stood and felt anger rising in her. She stared at him with her glowing blue eyes, a glower on her face. A figure appeared in her peripheral vision, but she ignored it.

Suddenly, the taps exploded and beer rained everywhere.

"Son of a bitch!" the bartender exclaimed, "What in the hell?!"

The guy looked at his wet suit and turned his head slightly and saw the figure.

Two light bulbs exploded, and a bottle of Jameson shattered.

"We're done." he said, "For now." he growled, looking between her and the figure.

He stormed out of the bar, squishing all the way. The figure on the edge of her vision came up to her.

It was Matthew.

"I came in here for beer, and I got it." he said, chuckling.

"My outfit is ruined." Rayna murmured, half-smiling.

"Look, my apartment is right around the corner. We'll go over there and clean up."

"I guess that's okay..." Rayna trailed off.

Her aunt's words stirred in her mind. But she pushed them aside. How bad could he be?

Matthew looked out the window and saw the man's eyes glow red for a second. He glared at him, and a streetlight outside exploded. The man muttered something and stalked off.

"Lots of explosions tonight." Rayna said as Matthew opened the door for her.

"It is Salem." he said, chuckling.

"We're not that weird." she argued, trying to stifle a smile.

"Come on. The Addams Family would move here with joy." Matthew said.

"There's more to us than that..." Rayna dropped off.

"Sarcasm." he reminded her.

"A weapon for those avoiding closeness." she countered, smirking.

"Touche." Matthew said.

He offered her his arm. She took it with hesitance.

* * *

They walked up the street and right around the corner to his apartment door. Matthew walked her up and unlocked the door, opening it to a very traditional colonial style place. Rayna saw a fire in the fireplace and wondered why he left it lit.

"Feel free to use the shower. Just toss your clothes outside the door, and I'll rinse & dry them. My daughter has girly bath stuff in there." he offered.

"Thanks." she replied.

"Second door on the right." he directed.

Rayna went in, closed the door, and threw her clothes outside. As Matthew heard the water run, he couldn't help but think about her wet body, the softness of her curves, her curly hair dripping with water, her full lips begging to be kissed. The fire crackled and spit embers. He shook his head and went into the bedroom, digging out a robe and some clothes from the closet.

"I'm done!" she called.

"Here's a robe." he said, holding it next to the door and turning his head.

Rayna grabbed it and closed the door. Within a minute, she stepped out. He gazed at her.

"You look good wet." Matthew said, smirking.

"Yeah, did I look as good wet with beer?" Rayna joked.

"Well, there was that smell…" he trailed off.

They both laughed.

"I'll be out in ten minutes." he said, going into the bathroom with some clothes.

As Matthew showered, Rayna browsed his family pictures on the bookshelf. A baby picture of his daughter. A photo of the family with his wife. She noticed the books on his shelf, many occult books and one dream dictionary.

Rayna cocked her head.

Matthew emerged from the bathroom in sweatpants and a Finn Balor t-shirt.

"Here, have a seat." he said, patting the couch.

Rayna heard the dryer tumbling.

"You take this Salem stuff seriously." she speculated.

"When you move here, you naturally have to check out the culture." Matthew replied.

"True," she agreed, fidgeting.

"I was most interested in the witch trials. So many innocent women were killed. And men and children." Matthew said in a soft voice.

"Yeah, when I was growing up, I learned about it. But I think it's just something we sell to the tourists." Rayna added, her eyes starting to glow.

"If only people would learn from their mistakes – though witchcraft isn't as persecuted so violently now." he reminded her.

A tear fell from her face.

"Why are you crying?" Matthew asked.

"I don't know…" Rayna said, confused.

"It's natural to feel that." he said.

He wiped the tear from her cheek.

They gazed at each other.

Water started dripping from the faucet in the kitchen.

"Hey Dad – I...." Rose greeted, bursting in the door.

She saw both of them wet, Rayna in a robe, and Rose's cheeks reddened.

"Um...did I miss something?" she asked.

"No no no..." Matthew furiously explained, "It's just...there was an accident at the bar, and we needed to dry our clothes."

He went to the dryer and took out her clothes.

"Here they are." Matthew excused, handing them to her.

"I'll be right out." Rayna said, going into the bathroom and closing the door.

She came out three minutes later, dressed.

"Thank you for the hospitality." Rayna said, opening the door.

"I hope we meet again...without beer everywhere." Matthew said, chuckling.

"Yeah, no more exploding alcohol." she agreed, smiling.

Matthew watched out the door as she walked down the stairs.

The fire roared.

"Dad...it's happening again." Rose warned, looking at the fireplace.

He took a deep breath.

The fire calmed.

Matthew collapsed on the couch.

When could he ever control it?

* * *

Salem 1692

"Do you plead guilty of witchcraft?" the judge asked, glaring at her.

"Yes, I do," she admits, "I made the girls go into hysteria for revenge. I was angry for the way I was treated."

"And how were you treated? Like the slave you are?" the judge asked, narrowing his eyes.

"I can't say, Your Honor."

"You were honest. Are you sorry?" he concluded.

"Yes. I promise to give up my ways."

"Very well. You and your husband will be sold to the highest bidder. Next case!" The judge ordered.

Samuel's eyes lit sparks as he saw her being led back to her quarters at his homestead.

She would pay.

Chapter Six

Rayna stopped at the bakery and ordered a mocha latte with a bacon and egg croissant sandwich. She strolled the streets as she took hungry bites and gulps the coffee. She reached their shop and tossed the wrapper and cup in the garbage.

Nakiyah was at the counter, stocking various sizes of sage bags. She turned around and stared at Rayna. Her eyes were glowing blue. Nakiyah shook a little as she closed the cabinet.

"How was your night?" she asked, averting her gaze.

"It was okay," Rayna said, looking at the orders on the counter, "Didn't meet anyone. Maybe next time."

Nakiyah squinted her eyes.

"The bar was quoted as saying there were accidents there last night in the daily paper," Nakiyah mentioned, "They said beer was everywhere."

"Yeah...something happened." Rayna admitted, casting her eyes down.

Nakiyah walked over to her and grabbed her shoulders firmly.

"Anger is destructive. Learn to channel it. I'm telling you this because I love you." she said.

She disappeared into the shelves, looking at the lists and grabbing books.

Rayna helped a few customers as they come in, doling out herbs and rose water – someone bought a cauldron, which Rayna offered to help carry to her car – and several people came to the counter with a few books.

'Business is good in Salem.'

The store quieted down, and Rayna noticed a thick, worn leather-bound book hidden underneath the counter. Her eyes darted around the store. She picked it up and opened it.

The History, it read on the title page.

It was dated in the 1600's.

Rayna turned the page and saw the words *love spell* before Nakiyah snatched it.

"You must never read this!" she exclaimed.

"Why? It can't be dangerous."

"No, but...you're not ready yet. When it's time, I'll tell you."

Nakiyah stuck it in a locked drawer and slipped the key in her bra.

"These customers will be coming in," she said, motioning to the books on the counter, "Just package the books. They paid on the website"

Nakiyah walked back into the stacks with more lists.

The bell jingled.

Rayna looked up and saw Matthew.

"You can't be here!" she hissed, "My aunt is back there!"

"I just came in for a few things," he said, "I need high john root, mint oil, and a drawstring bag."

Rayna grabbed the items quickly and swiped his card. She began to bag them but he insisted he would just take them. Matthew opened the plastic bag, taking out the high john root. He sprinkled it with mint oil and placed it in the bag, wearing it on a chain around his neck.

"What the hell is that for?" Rayna asked.

"Protection. And for overcoming obstacles."

"Like what?" she asked.

"Your aunt for one," he said with a smirk, "I'd like to see more of you."

Nakiyah walked up to the counter, double-checking the titles of the books, looked up, and saw Matthew.

Her eyes became milky white. She eyed the bag around his neck.

"Wise." Nakiyah said with simplicity.

"I'll see you around, Rayna." Matthew said, kissing her hand and eyeing her aunt.

He walked out, looking back at Rayna as he headed down the street.

"I told you to stay away from him! What really happened last night?!" Nakiyah exclaimed.

"I'm 34! You can't control me! He's kind, and he has a lovely daughter! Maybe he IS right for me – I'll decide on my own!" Rayna yelled back.

"I'm just trying to protect you." Nakiyah explained.

"From what?!" Rayna insisted.

"You don't know everything..." Nakiyah trailed off.

"Then tell me for Christ's sake! First there's some forbidden book and now this?! What the hell is going on?!" Rayna screamed.

The top of the glass counter shattered.

Nakiyah was left with her mouth agape.

"Nakiyah please..." Rayna pleaded with tears in her eyes, "Tell me."

"...I can't. Not yet." Nakiyah murmured with sadness in her voice, "I'm going to do inventory. I expect I'll be back there all day."

She dragged herself back to the stock room, her shoulders slumped.

Rayna's eyes glowed blue, but tears fell.

A bottle of rose water shattered on the floor and spilled.

Rayna grabbed a rag from under the counter and wiped up the water, carefully handling the shards of glass and putting them in the wastebasket.

Confusion clouded her brain like fog on a humid, rainy day.

She picked up the phone and called the company that sold them the display case. This would be a big bill. Thank God they could afford it. But it didn't give her any relief.

After the call, she turned the closed sign to the outside and grabbed her bag, exiting the store, leaving a note for her aunt. She needed space.

* * *

Salem 1692

She rubbed her wrists after they were released from the chains. John rushed over to her, hugging her and kissing her forehead.

"What did they say?" he asked.

"We are to be sold." she admitted.

"Will we be together?" John asked.

"I hope so." she replied.

"Here," he said, handing her a mug, "Lavender tea."

"I promised to give it up." she confessed.

"It's your heritage!" John argued.

"I had to, otherwise they would've burned or drowned me."

"Heavens forbid." he murmured, pulling her close.

They heard a thud outside the door. She looked out the window and saw a tree had snapped in half, blocking the door. She also saw him, staring with glowing red eyes at their house.

"We have to get out!" she exclaimed.

"What's wrong?" John asked.

"He has the Devil in his eyes. We have to go!"

Suddenly, fire rushed in the windows and engulfed the house. She and John knelt on the floor, clutching each other.

"I love you, my beloved," John said, "We perish together."

"I wouldn't have it any other way." she lied, kissing him with forced passion.

Her last thoughts were of her and Samuel kissing, caressing, murmuring words of love to each other. Tears fell down her cheeks.

In a few minutes, fire engulfed her and John. Their screams echoed in the village.

By the time the villagers got there, there was nothing but ashes – and the skeletons of their burned bodies, still clutching each other. In the back of the crowd was Samuel.

He smiled. Her bloodline would be destroyed.

Chapter Seven

Rayna entered a colonial store. She walked over to a table of handmade soap. She picked up each bar of soap and inhaled, searching for the right one.

"I guess you're looking for special stuff too." she heard a female voice say.

She looked and saw Rose, with her father trailing behind.

Rose tapped away on her smartphone, then shoved it in her pocket.

"Looking for something to attract love?" she snarked, raising an eyebrow.

"No...relaxation." Rayna answered, shifting her shoulders.

"Sorry about the attitude," Matthew said, walking over, "She was very close to her mother. Any woman that comes within a yard of me...she hates."

"It's okay, I was probably that way too once." Rayna admitted.

"Single parent?" he asked.

"More like single aunt. My parents died." Rayna explained, not going any further.

"I didn't want to share my aunt," she expounded, "She taught me everything that school didn't."

"Sounds like she was a good parent." Matthew commented.

"She's just...very protective."

"She might have reason or maybe not. It's a flip of the coin." he brushed off, running a hand through his hair.

Rayna picked up a purple bar with herbs inside. She sniffed it and handed it to Rose.

"Spearmint and Rosemary. Very relaxing and smells amazing." she said.

"Do you want to go look at shampoo?" Rayna asked Rose, grabbing a bar of gardenia soap.

Rose rolled her eyes, mumbled an answer, and skulked over to the display of bottles.

"I made her break a date to come here," Matthew said, "The guy wore a Cannibal Corpse shirt, jeans falling down his ass, and chains hanging from his pockets. And his face looked like a pin cushion."

"You made a good decision." Rayna said.

They opened and sniffed the different shampoos, Rayna choosing eucalyptus and Rose choosing vanilla.

"You know," Rayna nudged Rose, "If your dad is footing the bill, there's some plush bath towels in the back." she said with a smirk.

"At least there's that." Rose grumbled, stalking to the back of the aisle.

"I think you just cost me a shit ton more." Matthew said, laughing.

"So why the high john root?" Rayna asked, "I know you said protection, but from what?"

"I read about it in a book," he brushed off, "It protects you from evil and hexes."

"Who would hex you?" she asked.

"You never know." he said.

"I'm sorry about my aunt," Rayna apologized, "She's rough around the edges, but she has good intentions."

"I have yet to see the nice side of your aunt." he said.

"She hides it." Rayna said.

"So how about paninis and coffee at the Moonlight Cafe?" he asked, "I guess you love coffee."

"Gee, how'd you know?" she joked.

"By the cup you almost dropped in front of me when we first met." Matthew said, grinning.

Rose brought her items to the counter – including an expensive bath towel and washcloth – and Matthew swiped his credit card. He handed the bag to Rose, and they walked to the cafe, Rose texting on her phone and smiling.

Rayna knew she was only a teenager.

She just hoped it didn't get her into trouble.

* * *

Rayna sipped her peppermint mocha, before taking a bite of her chicken caprese panini. Matthew ordered the roast beef half sub, and Rose ordered a caesar salad. Matthew got black coffee, and Rose got green tea.

"So, who is this special guy?" Rayna asked Rose.

"Just a guy." she said firmly.

"Then why the smile?" Rayna asked.

"None of your business." Rose muttered.

"Well what's he into?" Rayna pushed.

"Um...stuff." Rose left it.

"Stuff...sounds interesting." Rayna snarked back, sipping her coffee.

"I can't believe they have holiday lattes out now." Matthew complained, shaking his head.

"If I could put my tree up now, I would." Rayna said.

"You run a witchy bookstore." he argued.

"Hey, Christmas trees started out as a Pagan tradition. And I'm an eclectic spiritual. I give honor to all beliefs. I just don't practice any." she argued.

"God!" Rose exclaimed, shoving her phone in her pocket.

"What's wrong honey?" Matthew asked.

"Julia can't come to our...get together....tonight." Rose said.

"What kind of get together?" Matthew asked, raising an eyebrow.

"Just a study group," Rose lied, "We have a history exam and project due next week."

"What topic?"

"The Trials. We are doing the first witch that ever confessed."

"Tituba?" Rayna asked.

"Yeah, how'd you know?" Rose asked.

"I snuck out to the tourist attractions when I was a teenager. I grew up with my aunt working nights in a restaurant, and she refused to educate me on the Trials, " she explained, "So I went to the dungeon and play with my friends.."

"So you know everything there is to know?" Rose asked.

"Yup. Just don't tell my aunt." Rayna whispered.

Matthew grinned.

"Maybe we could do that tonight," Rose wondered.

"Halloween *is* around the corner," Rayna paused, "As long as it's okay with your dad."

"Sounds like a terrifying time to me," he agreed, "I say go. I'll give you money for admission."

"Thanks Dad," Rose said, tapping away on her phone.

"You saved the night," Matthew whispered to Rayna.

"I had a feeling something bad was gonna happen. And I just happened to have the knowledge to help her." Rayna whispered back.

"Well...since she's gonna be out tonight...do you want to go to dinner?" he asked, "I have to thank you somehow."

"That would be nice, except I'm working tonight. Nakiyah is driving over to a dance club a few towns over with her friends." Rayna explained.

"How about I stop by?" he asked, "Then she can't freeze me with her glare."

"There's something about you..." he said, confusion clouding his eyes.

"Yeah...I feel the same way." Rayna agreed, trying to read his expression.

"So...how about tomorrow after school you come over and tell me about Tituba?" Rose asked, interrupting them and smirking.

"Sure. I can come by and give you the low down. I just hope it helps."

"I need the A. I'm coasting with a C this semester." Rose said with a sigh.

Rayna downed the last of her coffee and threw the cup out.

"I'm gonna head off to the gym. I need to work off my lunch." she said, slipping her jacket on.

"Are you working out in that?" Matthew asked, " 'Cause if so, you'll look good."

She chuckled.

"I'll send you a selfie of me in my workout gear so you can see how hardcore I am." she replied, smiling.

They exchanged cell phone numbers.

"I'll see you tonight." Matthew said, shaking her hand.

His hand went burning hot – while her hand was cool.

"See you later." she said.

As she walked to her apartment to change, she lowered her head.

Was her aunt right?

Chapter Eight

Salem – 1982

A caramel skinned woman in torn jeans and a t-shirt tied in a knot to show off her toned abs walked down the street, earphones on her head. She closed her eyes for a second and crashed into someone. She opened her eyes and saw a Caucasian man, auburn hair, blue eyes, and wearing a black button-down shirt.

"I'm sorry." she apologized, looking at his spilled groceries.

Both of them crouched down to re-bag the food.

"What were you listening to?" he asked.

"'I Hate Myself For Loving You'." she replied, smiling.

"Interesting." he said, standing up, clutching his paper bag of groceries.

She looked in his eyes and then closed hers - she saw him playing with an acoustic band in a bar in Ireland.

"You're Irish?" she asked, opening her eyes.

"How did you know?" he asked surprised.

"Women's intuition." she said, smirking.

"I actually just moved from the Green Isle. I switched jobs for a steadier income." he replied.

"Where are you working?" she asked.

"At a curiousity shop a few blocks away," he said.

"Well, as an apology for knocking over your food...here." she said, handing him a business card.

"Your number?" he asked, smiling.

"Yeah. You're cute." she said, smirking.

"How about dinner at my place?" she asked.

Her eyes glowed blue. As he stared into them, water exploded from the fountain in the square.

"What the hell was that?" he asked.

"Must be a pipe malfunction..." she trailed off.

"Are you asking me on a date?" he asked rhetorically, smiling.

"Maybe," she flirted, "After all, you just went shopping."

"Oh...so you want me to cook dinner?" he asked, raising an eyebrow.

She was silent, her eyes focused on his.

"So?" he asked again.

She grabbed him by the collar of his shirt, kissing him passionately and running her fingers through his hair. He wrapped his hands in her curls, dropping his bag, and reaching down, caressing her ass and pulling her against him.

He pulled away, breathless.

"Christ...I'd have done that sooner if all I had to do was drop my groceries." he said breathlessly.

"Tonight at 6?" she asked, dabbing at her lips in case her red lipstick smeared.

"Yeah. Whatever you want." he said, grabbing her hand and pulling her to him.

"Uh-uh..." she warned, pulling away, "You have to wait til tonight."

"Fine. Absence makes the heart grow fonder."

"And that bulge in your pants." she said, giggling.

He blushed and pulled his shirt down.

"Not doing much." she said, putting her hand over his heart, "Let me try to help."

He felt a coolness fill his chest and spread throughout his body. The heat inside him died down, and he felt calm & centered.

"How'd you do that?" he asked, incredulous.

"Secret." she said, pecking him on the lips, "See you at 6. Make me chicken cacciatore."

"How did you know I was gonna make that?" he asked.

She shrugged and smiled.

As she put her earphones back on and walked down the street with a bounce in her steps. The music thudded through her ears -

"I hate myself for loving you

Can't break free from the things that you do

I wanna walk but I run back to you
That's why
I hate myself for loving you"
He turned around and watched her, smiling. Not a bad view. And,
apparently, there was more to her than met the eye.

* * *

Rayna stared at the newspaper article she kept in her memory box. The headline read, *"House fire kills two – child survives".* Rayna read through the article over and over through the years. They said it was spontaneous combustion from some kind of appliance.

Three white pillar candles were lit and on candle pedestals on the counter. She eyed them with wariness. She just smudged with white sage, trying to clear the negativity and tension from the shop. She took out her wallet and gazed at a photo in the side pocket – her mother, her father, and her as a baby. They looked so happy.

Rayna almost dropped her wallet. She quickly grabbed it mid-air and shoved it in her front pocket. She wiped away the tears that dripped down her face.

The door of the shop jingled. She looked up and saw Matthew.

"Quiet." he commented.

"Yeah, this is the peaceful part of my day." Rayna said, sipping her cup of tea.

Matthew took a deep inhale.

"What kind of tea is that?" he asked.

"Rose hips and lavender. It's said to bring peace and attract love." she said with a faint smile.

"You sound a little witchy." he said jokingly.

"Nah, I never practiced anything." she lied in part, seeing her spell work.

"Even as a child?" he asked.

"My mom taught me how to make teas and taught me how to bake these special breads & pastries. I was only six." she explained.

"Your mom sounds like she was very caring. I wish my parents were. I was always different and...as an adult..it got worse." Matthew lamented.

"Different isn't bad," Rayna insisted, "I'm different too."

"Looks like we're a good pair." he said, smiling.

"Time will tell," Rayna said, moving herb jars around in the cabinet, "I don't rush into anything anymore."

"Would it be rushing in if I kissed you?" Matthew asked with a gentle tone.

"I think so," she replied, "We would need a date first."

"Okay, so how about I take you to that bistro a few blocks away, and we have a gourmet dinner and some wine?" he asked.

"You're not trying to take advantage of me, are you?" she asked.

"No, I just know the best wines. My uncle has a vineyard in California. I thought you'd enjoy a good vintage."

"The good ones always cost the moon." she commented.

"Hey, I'm not broke, and I'm not a millionaire either. I can afford a good bottle of wine and a nice meal for two." Matthew insisted.

"Okay, you wore me down." Rayna admitted.

"Tomorrow at six?" he asked.

"I'll see you then." she said, a glow on her face.

"Well, I gotta go wait for Rose to get home. I'm hoping she got enough information for her report. Thanks again."

"You're welcome. Let me know how she liked it." Rayna said.

Matthew leaned over and kissed her cheek, leaving a warm feeling there.

"Tomorrow night," Matthew said, "I'll sweep you off your feet."

"I've heard that before." Rayna replied, smirking.

"Yeah, but you never heard it from me." he replied, grinning.

"Touche. See you then."

As Matthew left and walked down the street, he felt the heat rise in him. He started taking deep breaths to calm himself, but before he knew it, another streetlight exploded.

He looked down at the sidewalk with a frustrated glare.

Could he control it tomorrow night?

* * *

Rayna sat on Rose's daybed with her the next day, aged books scattered across the bed, Rose typing on her laptop. The room smelled of white sage.

"White sage?" Rayna asked.

"...I've been smudging," Rose admitted, "I read about it in one of my father's books. It cleanses the house of negativity."

"Is there negativity here?" Rayna asked.

"I don't know," Rose lied, "I just want me and my dad to stay protected."

"Wow," Rayna mused, "This is the first you've opened up to me."

Rose rolled her eyes.

"Well, I figured I owed you for the help. Don't make a big deal out of it."

She went back to scanning the books, typing away for her report.

"So what happened to Tituba?" Rose asked.

"No one knows. It wasn't documented," Rayna replied, "The only thing we know is her and her husband were sold off together to another owner."

"What if we found out?" Rose asked.

"It's impossible without some kind of historical record." Rayna admitted.

"Do you think she was happy after the trial?" Rose inquired.

"No, I don't think so," Rayna said with sadness, "Even being with her husband...the trial had to leave traumatic memories. They tortured people in those days to get them to confess. Giles Cory had a board put

2

on top of him, and each time he denied it, they added another boulder until it crushed him."

Rose's mouth dropped open.

"Some witches were drowned, hanged, and burned at the stake," Rayna continued, "A lot of innocent women, men, and children died. It was pure hysteria. But it didn't last too long. Eventually the hunt stopped. It's a bad memory that still lives on to this day."

A tear dropped down Rose's face. Rayna wiped it away.

"That's why so many tourists come to Salem. They want to see all the shops, selling witchcraft wares, spell books, and Trial histories," Rayna added, "So don't feel too upset. Some people are more open-minded now."

Rayna choked on tears.

"Is witchcraft Satanic?" she asked.

"Witches don't believe in Satan. I've read the introductory books in my spare time for education." Rayna replied.

"That guy I was meeting...he's...dark. He invited me to a bonfire..." Rose began, "I was going to, but I didn't want to be like him. I'm glad my dad dragged me off to that bath shop, and you told me about the places in town."

"Does he belong to a group?" Rayna asked.

"He says it's just a group of friends that gets together and parties."

"I think it's a great thing you followed your inner guidance." Rayna replied.

"I appreciate...you looking out for me." Rose said.

"Would it be okay if I hugged you?" Rayna asked softly.

Rose nodded. Rayna wrapped her arms around her and focused her thoughts & heart on sending love and comfort to her.

When Rose pulled away, she had a half-smile.

"Now let's finish this report. Here's a book on the other victims of the Trials. What do you think you can do with that?" Rayna asked.

Rose paused in thought.

"Compare Tituba to those who didn't confess?"

"There you go." Rayna concluded, "Your father and I are going out now, but keep studying."

Rayna walked out and closed the door.

Matthew was in the living room in a black button down shirt, black jacket & pants, and black loafers. He wore the cloth bag around his neck, but it was tucked beneath his shirt.

He looked at Rayna. She was wearing a pink, long skirt with sequins and embroidery at the bottom and a pink, flowered draped top with plain wedges.

"God, you look gorgeous." he said, breathless.

"You look good too." she said, blushing.

"Shall we?" he asked, offering her his arm.

She took it, and they headed out of the house. He opened the door to his 2018 black Honda Civic and helped her in, even buckling her seatbelt. He closed the door and got in his side, turning on the engine.

"Get ready for a meal you will never forget." he said, grinning.

"I'm ready." she said, smiling back.

They drove down the street, heading into town.

In the book shop, Nakiyah was clutching her head and shrieking. She saw them together.

The worst happened.

* * *

Salem – 2006

Matthew sat in an uncomfortable chair – hard-backed, with a beat up cushion – watching his wife. She breathed in and out slowly and with shallowness, every exhale a whimper. There was a morphine drip set up.

He fed her sorbet and ice cream from a spoon and gave her sips of water, so she got something inside her.

He put his head in his hands.

"I'd do anything for you to go peacefully..." he whispered.

A doctor stood in the doorway that he didn't see.

"I heard what you just said," he addressed him, giving him a startle, "And I can help you."

"How?" he exclaimed.

"She will go in peace. No pain."

He extended his hand.

The husband started to extend his hand, withdrew it for a moment, and then shook the doctor's hand, feeling a burn.

Suddenly his wife mouthed his name. He turned to her, but the man kept the grip on his hand. Her eyes opened for a split second, before she fell into a deep sleep.

Suddenly, she was engulfed in flames, the fire burning every remnant of her body, nothing left. The bed was empty and made. The IV was gone.

He jumped up, pulling away his hand.

"What did you do?!" he shouted.

"She went peacefully." the doctor replied with a toothy grin.

The husband felt a burning in his body. He glared at the doctor.

The walls burst into flames, setting off the smoke alarm.

"What the hell?!" the husband exclaimed.

"This is yours now. Welcome." the doctor said, his facade gone, as he appeared in a black striped suit with a red tie, his hair slicked back, his eyes glowing red.

"What have I done?" the husband whispered.

The husband ran out of the hospital as the orderlies attacked the fire with extinguishers.

The man disappeared and faded into nothing as the orderlies's backs were turned.

As he descended into Hell, he smiled.

This one would end it.

* * *

Rayna sat at a table with a pristine white tablecloth and silver flatware, her wine glass filled with white wine – a Pinot Grigio. Matthew had a glass of whiskey on the rocks. They were perusing the menu.

"What will you prefer?" the server asked.

"I'll have the wild duck salad before my entree," Rayna ordered, "And the lamb chops."

"I'll have the escargot for an appetizer, and the prime rib for my entree." Matthew said.

As the server walked away, Rayna blushed.

"You can afford all this?" she asked.

"Yeah. I got a pay raise at work because the products I've been selecting have been flying off the shelves." he replied, putting a hand on hers.

She felt a burn in his hand and a coolness in hers.

Together they produced an electric current between them.

"So tell me something about yourself." she insisted.

"Well...I was on the debate team in high school. I defended issues like immigration, women's rights, and a raised minimum wage – while my opponents defended pro-lifers, kicking out immigrants, and attacked the rights of victims of sexual assault."

"Hm. Ominous." Rayna commented, leaning her head on her hand.

"Yeah, pretty much. Other than that, I was in the choir, I played guitar, and I took home ec to learn how to cook so I could provide for a family one day." Matthew added.

"You sound like a character in a book." she joked.

"Well, I'm not Romeo, but I could be Cory Booker."

"I don't know if he plays guitar and sings." she said, smiling.

"Well, let's pretend he does." Matthew said, smiling back, "So tell me about you."

"Well...my parents...died when I was six. Then my aunt took over as my guardian. She became another mother to me. She wouldn't let me look into the Trials, like I told Rose. So I would go to the library after school. At night, my friends and I would have 'sleepovers' and go to the Salem attractions," she explained.

"They gave you nightmares afterwards." Rayna added with a half-smile.

"Something tells me you have more invested in this." he commented.

"I'm just drawn to it. I don't know why." she said, zoning out into the restaurant window.

"I'm drawn to you." Matthew said, grinning.

"Me too." Rayna said, giving him a grin back.

As their appetizers arrived, Rayna dug into her salad, and Matthew ate his escargot.

* * *

Meanwhile, Nakiyah ran to Rayna's apartment and unlocked the door, entering.

"Rayna!!" she yelled.

No answer. She left and locked the door. She ran to the bookstore only to see a dark shop. And she noticed a bottle of rose oil missing from the shelf.

"Fuck!" she exclaimed.

She was running down a few blocks, when something told her to look in the restaurant next to her. There were Rayna and Matthew, their hands clasped. Both of them whispering to each other.

"Oh My God!" she nearly yelled.

She ran inside, grabbed Rayna by the arm, and dragged her outside.

"What are you doing?!" Rayna shouted.

"You can't be with that man!!" Nakiyah yelled.

"Why?!" Rayna exclaimed.

"Um....because....he's white!"

"Yeah, I noticed that." Rayna replied, dripping with sarcasm.

"He's not right for you!! I've seen it!" Nakiyah insisted.

"What do you mean by, "you've seen it"?" Rayna asked.

"Look, I just sense he's trouble. You don't need that in your life."

"I'm an adult," Rayna said calmly, "I live on my own, I pay my own bills, and I own 51% of the shop because you insisted on that. Stay out of my personal business." she warned, eyes beginning to narrow.

"Rayna, calm down," Nakiyah said, putting a hand on her shoulder, You don't know everything."

"What don't I know? You're speaking in riddles." Rayna asked, taking a deep breath.

"Mark my words, this won't end well." Nakiyah warned.

"I'll find that out for myself," Rayna ended the argument, "Go back home or go dancing."

She went back into the restaurant and sat down.

Nakiyah's head started to pound and ache.

There was no stopping it now.

She had to find out on her own.

* * *

"Sorry about that," Rayna apologized, "My aunt seems to be a bit controlling."

"A bit?" Matthew asked, raising an eyebrow.

"She's just worried about me," Rayna explained, "But I can see who you are. You're kind – compassionate – well-cultured – we share the same beliefs."

"I can see you," he said, "You're strong-willed, independent, and you don't take shit from anyone," he paused.

"Maybe she should be worried about me." he added, chuckling.

"I'm not worried about either of us." she replied, a glow in her cheeks.

"Neither am I." he whispered.

They talked about their years in high school, growing up, and the whole Salem kitsch as they had dinner. He paid the check, and he drove her home.

When they got to her doorstep, she paused at the door and turned to him.

"Would you like to come in for a nightcap?" she asked, blushing.

"I shouldn't," he excused himself, "It should happen when it's right."

"Then how about this?" she asked, kissing him.

He kissed her gently at first, but then he pulled her to him, devouring her mouth.

The candles in her house became lit.

She felt something like water rushing over her, filling her with a love she had never known before.

The tub began to run water.

Rayna pulled away, breathless.

"I should go." she said, taking his hand.

"How about we go to the cafe tomorrow morning an hour before work?" Matthew asked, "We can grab coffee and breakfast and get to know more about each other."

"How about coffee here?" she offered, "I make great banana nut bread, and I have an espresso machine."

"Even better." he said, pecking her on the lips, "I just have to drop Rose at school first."

"See you here at eight?" she asked.

"You know it." he said, smirking.

As Matthew turned around, she patted his ass.

"Haven't felt that in a while." he called as he walked away.

Rayna laughed and went inside closing the door.

She saw the candles burning and heard the running water.

She ran to the bathroom, where the tub was full of water, and turned it off.

She gazed into the water and noticed her container of rose petals and bottle of rose water on the shelf.

It seemed to be working...

...time for another rose bath.

* * *

That night, Matthew bolted out of sleep.

He knew what his memory was protecting him from.

He knew what he was.

"Finish what I started." a voice whispered in the room.

Matthew felt his anger rise, and the fire lit in the fireplace, sparking and rising wildly.

"Dad!!" he heard his daughter yell.

He felt his anger calm, and he ran down stairs. He saw the fire, now calmer and more warm & comforting than threatening.

"It was happening again." Rose said with a shudder.

"It's never gonna destroy anything ever again," Matthew said, hugging her with a spark in his eyes, "I'm not gonna become what others want."

"But...what about West Orange?" Rose asked, "The apartment that burned?" she asked.

"It will NEVER happen again." he emphasized, "I'm not that person. I will never be."

"Yes, you will. You're mine." a voice whispered in his ear.

"Why don't you go up to bed?" Matthew asked, "Then you can explain why you were out so late."

Rose trudged up the stairs to her room.

Matthew sat on the couch, gazing into the fireplace.

How would he ever tell Rayna?

How would she ever believe what he said?

And how would they ever survive the truth?

* * *

Salem 1992

"Daniel!" she yelled, "You were out again! I'm up to my elbows in laundry, the dishes need to be rinsed and put in the dishwasher, and the garbage needs to go out! Not to mention someone has to play with Rayna!"

"I need to get away from all this shit," he mumbled, taking a drag of a cigarette.

"What happened to you?" she asked, tears in her eyes, "It's like some new side of you came out. "

"Maybe." he said, stubbing out the cigarette on the side table.

"That was my grandmother's table!" she yelled.

"Watch it, I'm warning you..." he said, raising his hand.

"What have you become?" Josie asked.

"I'm your worst nightmare," he growled, his eyes turning red,"I finally have the power I deserve in this house."

Rayna looked up from her Barbie dolls and the kitchen playset. She never saw her daddy that angry.

"Nakiyah!" Josie screamed.

Nakiyah came running from the bathroom where she was running a bath for Rayna.

"Get her out of here! Just run!" Josie yelled.

Nakiyah grabbed Rayna's stuffed rabbit and grabbed her, covering Rayna's eyes as she ran out the door to her car. She took out her car phone and dialed 911.

Rayna heard screams.

She looked at the house, saw a tree fall against the door, and the windows slam closed, shutters and all.

She saw flames engulf the entire house.

"Mommy!" Rayna screamed, reaching for the door.

Nakiyah grabbed her and strapped her in the child seat in the back. She took off, screeching the tires, smoke blowing behind them.

Rayna wailed as they drove off, missing her mother.

'It's true, it's all true...' Nakiyah thought, her eyes wide and her body trembling.

Chapter Nine

Rayna strolled the cobblestone streets with Matthew, chewing on a candy apple. Matthew ate popcorn from a red-striped bag. They had just come from an outdoor concert. It was some band that did covers of alternative songs. Rayna grimaced. It was the guy from the bar.

"I really wish they would actually stick to the core of Foo Fighters." Rayna said.

"Yeah, they're ruining good music." Matthew replied, grimacing.

They stopped at a table with jewelery made from recycled paper. Rayna turned and saw her aunt glaring at them from the bookstore window and mumbling with her lips. Matthew noticed her diverted attention and turned around.

"Is your aunt putting a curse on me?" he asked.

"No, she's just probably muttering F words under her breath." Rayna said, smirking.

"I care about you. Doesn't she get that?" Matthew asked.

"She's just worried." Rayna said with a harsh exhale.

"About what?"

"She says I'm in danger, but I think she's delusional."

Matthew stayed silent for a second.

"I'm not dangerous," he murmured, "Just misunderstood."

"So am I," Rayna agreed, "She still sees me as that little helpless girl."

Rayna took a colorful paper bead necklace and handed the woman a five dollar bill.

She put it on, and they continued down the block.

"Wait, I see my favorite shop over there!" Rayna exclaimed.

"Which one is that?" Matthew asked, noticing a manhole behind her.

"The gemstone shop. I've been wanting a rainbow crystal." she said.

Matthew put his hand on her shoulder. A violent urge came over him.

He could push her, and she'd plummet – her body splattering in the sewer.

His eyes began to spark.

"Are you okay?" she asked.

The urge disappeared. Matthew pulled her towards him.

"I was just worried," he lied, pointing to the open manhole.

"Lord, I could've fallen and died!" Rayna exclaimed, putting her hand on her heart, feeling it racing.

"Yeah…" he trailed off, "Good thing I was here."

She wrapped her arms around his waist and laid her head on his chest.

"The more time I spend with you, the more I fall for you." Rayna whispered.

Matthew kissed her forehead. Then he tipped her head up and pecked her lips.

"I'd never let anything happen to you." he promised.

Matthew felt his pulse race as he said those words.

He'd push back those urges with every bit of strength he had.

* * *

The October wind blew Rose's long wavy dirty blonde hair into her face. She brushed it back and stared off into the distance as her boyfriend, Kyle, talked about the group he'd joined. She caught various phrases like "bonfires" and "drinks", but she was in her own world. Rose's brown eyes blazed with frustration.

This wasn't the relationship she'd hoped for.

"Hey…I asked if you wanted to come to our party tonight." Kyle said, nudging her.

"No, I have a lot of stuff to study. And I have to finish my paper."

"On those stupid Trials? They all deserved what they got." he mumbled, taking out what looked like a textbook and removing a flask, taking a swig. He quickly shoved it back into his backpack.

"How can you say that? They were innocent!" Rose argued, hands on her hips.

Kyle ran a hair through his hair, exhaling with depth.

"Look – I know you've become involved with these trials because of your father's girlfriend. It's okay to be interested, but you have to face facts."

"Witches aren't bad people!" Rose yelled, an amber swirl coming into her eyes.

A group of teenagers outside the school looked over.

"Quiet!" Kyle hushed.

"No! You are such a judgmental asshole!"

"I'm not! It's the truth!" Kyle exclaimed.

"NO. It's. Not!" she yelled.

Suddenly a tree snapped in half and almost hit Kyle, but he jumped out of the way.

"What the hell?!" he exclaimed.

A teacher rushed over.

"Are you two okay?" he asked.

"Yeah, we're fine." Rose said, shaking.

"That tree was 200 years old – it was bound to happen," the teacher said with a harsh breath.

"I gotta go," Rose said, grabbing her messenger bag, and rushing down the street.

"You shouldn't hang around here after school," the teacher told Kyle, "Who knows what can happen here?"

"I think I can handle it." Kyle said, looking him defiantly in the eyes.

He tugged on the collar of his leather jacket and stormed off.

He would get her there.

* * *

Rose nearly steamrolled through the door of the bookshop, panting with heaviness. Rayna looked at her, her blue eyes clouding with confusion.

"What's wrong?" Rayna asked.

"Something happened." Rose stammered, leaning on the counter for support, "I was arguing with my boyfriend and a tree snapped and almost hit him."

Alarm showed in Rayna's eyes as she remembered the glass breaking.

Nakiyah walked to the front and saw Rose, jumping back.

"What's wrong?" Rose asked her.

"Rayna, let me handle this." Nakiyah insisted, putting an arm around Rose's shoulder.

"But...you don't know her."

"Sometimes you know a person just by looking in their eyes," she began, "I wish YOU did."

Nakiyah walked Rose into the back office, Rayna rolling her eyes at her aunt.

* * *

Nakiyah sat Rose down and poured boiling water into a cup of lavender tea from a hot plate. Rose sipped it and felt her muscles relaxing.

"I know you must be confused..." Nakiyah trailed off.

"How do you know what happened?"

"I overheard." Nakiyah lied.

"It was so scary." Rose said, trembling.

"Have you been reading a lot lately?" Nakiyah asked her, looking deep in her eyes.

As Rose looked in her eyes, she felt comfort.

"I've been reading some of my dad's books. Just on..." she drifted.

"Witchcraft?" Nakiyah asked, raising an eyebrow.

"Yeah..." Rose admitted, surprised at her knowledge.

"I won't lie to you. I sensed your ability," Nakiyah began, "You're naturally gifted. And the fact a tree fell...your element is earth."

"Whoa...I can't handle this stuff." Rose said, starting to get up and shaking.

"Listen, please," Nakiyah pleaded, "I can help you."

"How?" Rose asked, tears in her eyes, "Danger surrounds my family."

"If you can control it and direct your power, you will only use your powers for good."

"What if...I'm in danger?" she asked.

"However you choose to use them at that precise moment is up to you."

"How can you help me?" Rose asked.

Nakiyah took a shaky breath and unlocked a drawer in her desk, taking out a leather-bound book.

"With this..." she paused...

"...I'm a witch, too."

Chapter Ten

Salem - 1990

Daniel sat in a bar, sipping a glass of whiskey on the rocks. His anger was raging.

"Daniel! Can you play with your daughter?"

"Can you cook dinner? I'm under a mountain of laundry."

"I need you to fix my car! I can't get to work. And you have to pick up your daughter after school."

"Stop smoking! That isn't good for her lungs!"

"Are you eating cold cuts again? You'll clog your arteries!"

He took a drag of his cigarette and rested it in the ash tray. He took another gulp of whiskey and slammed the glass down on the counter.

"Got some troubles?" a voice asked.

He looked next to him and saw a man in a black suit and red tie, salt and pepper hair slicked back, wearing a Rolex watch.

"Yeah," he mumbled in reply, "I got a wife and 7 year old daughter at home. Both pains in my ass. Not to mention her sister is over all the time."

"Oh, so you feel you're not in charge?" the man asked.

"She nags and when I don't do like I'm told, she yells. Usually glass breaks."

"That's unusual."

"My wife is very strange. So is her sister. I guess it's genetic because whenever my daughter screams, faucets run or it starts raining."

"Sounds like you need a break." the man suggested, sipping a glass of bourbon.

"I wish I could, man. I wish I never came to this godforsaken town."

"I can help you," the man offered, holding out his hand.

Daniel looked at his hand.

He shook the man's hand firmly, feeling a burn.

"It will be better." the man assured him.

"Thank. Well, gotta get home before the wife starts screaming again."
Daniel said, putting his suede jacket on.
"She will." the man said, smirking.
As Daniel left, the man chuckled.
"I could use the help, too." he said, baring a jagged grin.

* * *

Rose sat on her bed with the book Nakiyah gave her, confused.

Where did she get this power?

She knew Hermoine got her wizarding powers, even having two muggle parents.

Was she like Hermoine?

She took the white candle Nakiyah gave her, put it in a holder, and lit it for mental clarity. Rose sipped the lavender tea she bottled for her.

She opened the book with hesitance. She saw it dated 1690. When she saw the message inscribed and the signature, she gasped.

Rose shut it with immediacy.

She put on her jacket and ran to the front door.

"Where are you going?" Matthew asked, looking up from a stapled bunch of papers.

"I just need to see Rayna." she babbled, unlocking the door.

"It's nine o'clock. She closes at ten. Same time as your curfew."

"I'll be back by then." Rose promised.

Rose ran out the door and down the block, heading towards town. A hand grabbed her arm.

"Hey, did you forget about the party?" Kyle asked, his sandy blonde hair falling in his face, his hazel eyes intense.

"I have somewhere to go..." Rose said, trying to keep running.

"Come on, you can relax – have a drink – enjoy marshmallows roasted over a fire..." he enticed.

Rose felt her gut telling her not to go.

"I have to go. I'm sorry." she said, pulling free and running down the street.

Kyle's eyes burned red.

Someone appeared behind him out of nowhere and put a hand on his shoulder.

"She's one of them. Finish it." the voice growled.

"Yes, Samuel." Kyle answered.

As he stalked down the street, Samuel grinned.

The bloodline would end.

* * *

Rose rushed in the store like a hurricane force wind. Rayna looked up.

"More trouble?" she asked, curious.

"Rayna...I know what happened to Tituba."

"Wait...nothing was ever found about her..." Rayna trailed off.

"Your aunt gave me a book. It was signed by her."

"That's not possible..." Rayna said, backing against the cabinet.

"She wrote a message in there! It was for your family!"

"What do you mean *my* family?!" Rayna exclaimed, her blue eyes flaring.

"It said 'Keep this in the bloodline – we must survive.' "

Rayna froze.

"You're imagining things," she brushed off, trembling, "Today's accident shook you up."

Rose reached into her messenger bag and pulled out the book, opening to the first page. Rayna moved forward with timidity, analyzing the writing.

Her mouth dropped.

Rose was right.

"Holy -" she began.

She was cut off by a fire lighting in the book stacks. Rayna gasped. Rose looked and saw Kyle standing outside, his eyes glowing red.

"What the hell?!" Rose screamed.

Rayna's eyes glowed blue as she stared at Kyle out the window.

A pipe burst in the ceiling and water rushed out, putting out the fire.

Rose was hyperventilating. Rayna put her hand on her heart, and Rose's breathing slowed.

"How did you do that?" Rose asked.

"I don't know...I've been able to do it ever since I was a kid. I stopped a lot of fist fights that way on the playground."

They looked out the window again, and Kyle was gone.

"He knows where I live..." Rose trailed off, shaking.

"My question is, how did he do that?" Rayna replied, dialing the plumber.

"How are you gonna get a plumber this late?" Rose asked.

"I have connections."

"Nakiyah is gonna find out all this." Rose warned.

"Well, now, I have a feeling she won't be shocked." Rayna replied with an edge.

As the dial tone rung, she narrowed her eyes.

Nakiyah lied to her.

She just hoped whatever this was in her wouldn't drown her aunt

* * *

Salem – 1990

Josie handed Nakiyah a mug of tea. Then she went back to doctoring the stew she had in a cast iron pot on the stove. Nakiyah sipped her tea and eyed Josie.

"So you believe in the history?" she asked.

"I believe what Mom told us. She knew something was wrong." Josie said with a tear in her eye.

"At least we had Grandmother." Nakiyah consoled.

"Yes, she taught us the ways of our ancestry. Many's a time I have consulted this." she said, patting the leather-bound book on the table.

"Why do you re-read that diary over and over? You're just torturing yourself."

"I used some kitchen magick in this stew for calming. Daniel's been...on edge." Josie said, changing the subject.

She stirred the stew and added some herbs from small jars, stirring again.

"I'm sure it's stress from work," Nakiyah insisted, "He commutes to Boston to head a major penthouse building – nothing is more stressful than dealing with the public."

"I suppose," Josie accepted with reluctance, "But he's been arguing, not doing what I ask, yelling at Rayna."

"Look, that so-called history is myth. Mom and Dad's deaths were freak accidents." Nakiyah insisted, finishing her tea, "I'm gonna go run a bath for Rayna. Some lavender oil in it will calm her."

Rayna was crying in the corner, calling for her father.

"He'll be home soon," Nakiyah soothed, "He loves you so much."

As they disappeared into the bathroom, Josie felt hairs stiffen on her neck.

Something bad was coming.

* * *

Nakiyah stirred some rose hip and chamomile tea. She made two cups. She felt something strong. She closed her eyes and focused.

She saw everything that happened.

She unwrapped her banana nut bread, Rayna's favorite, and cut a slice – one for each plate.

Nakiyah looked at the yellow roses on the table.

She always bought yellow roses every two weeks and placed them in the center of the table she had in the center of the room, against the wall. It also had runes in a small bowl, a Goddess statue, a wooden pentacle, an altar cloth, and several reference books were on her bookshelf.

The door burst open, and Rayna stood there, soaked to the bone.

"I was expecting you." Nakiyah said with simplicity.

"You have a lot -"

"Of explaining to do. I know. Let me put your clothes in the dryer and you can put on one of my dresses."

She went in the bedroom with Rayna, undressed her, and slipped a purple dress over her head. She threw the clothes in the dryer and turned it on.

"Please, sit." Nakiyah offered, pulling out a chair.

Rayna looked at it with wariness and noticed the bread and tea on the table.

"You can't bribe me to calm down." She said in a deeper voice, her eyes sparking blue.

"I know you're upset, but let me tell you the story. Please." Nakiyah pleaded.

"Fine." Rayna huffed, sitting down.

Nakiyah told Rayna of Tituba's life story – everything she wrote in the book.

"This tragedy has repeated itself in our family for ages. Every time a woman in our family married a man, he ended up hating her – and killing them both in a fire..."

Nakiyah paused, looking down.

"I've seen the spark in your boyfriend's eyes. He's one of them. Please don't pursue him any further."

"You don't know that, and this sounds like a crock of bull." Rayna argued, pushing away her bread.

"You wanted to know what happened to her – and that's the truth. It's why your parents died."

"What do you mean?" she asked.

"Your father...caused the fire. Your mother collapsed the tree against the house and shut the windows. She wanted him to die – unable to kill you or me." Nakiyah explained.

Rayna sat there, her eyes filled with tears and confusion, her hands clasped together.

The teapot on the table began to crack.

"Control it," Nakiyah said, "This is your power."

"Wait – what do you mean this is my power?" Rayna asked.

"Water. It's why the bottles break, why the taps exploded, why the pipe broke. All contain some form of water. Your anger and sadness trigger it. You must learn to direct your power and harness it."

"I'm a – a – a witch?" Rayna stuttered.

"You must study the craft and accept your place. It's your choice. But you will always have the power." Nakiyah said, grasping her hand.

Rayna felt a coolness and a breeze came in the window, refreshing her.

"Strange, it wasn't windy before." Rayna observed.

"My power is air." Nakiyah explained, "If your boyfriend keeps studying the craft and overcomes the deal he made...he will be the fourth corner."

"What deal?"

Nakiyah froze.

Trees were on fire. A man in a black suit, red tie, and with salt and pepper hair stood in the middle of the clearing. Rose was pinned down. Matthew stood over Rayna, his red eyes glowing.

"Do it." Samuel commanded, "End the bloodline."

Matthew conjured a fireball in his hands and held it above his head.

Nakiyah clutched her head and shook it, stopping the vision.

"What's wrong?" Rayna asked, kneeling by her.

"The final confrontation will come. And your boyfriend will use his power."

"He wouldn't do that to me! He stopped me from falling down a manhole! He cares about my safety!"

"Rayna...Samuel chose him to end the bloodline."

"This is crazy..." Rayna trailed off.

"I saw it. You can ignore it if you want, but it's better to get him on our side."

"This whole history of women in our family burning...it's..." Rayna drifted.

"I know it sounds like something out of a horror novel, but it's true. I promise you."

"Rose has the diary..." Rayna trailed off.

"It has our history leading up to the 1900's. Ancestors through the years took it down – the ones who survived. This is the only proof I have." Nakiyah promised.

Rayna took the book, swaying a bit with dizzyness.

"You're clairvoyant..." Rayna said.

"I got it from our mother. Your mother had it too." Nakiyah said, a tear trailing down her cheek.

"What do we do?" Rayna asked with weakness.

"We fight."

Rayna sat there for a second.

"I'm heading home. I need time to take this all in."

"I understand. Just be careful." Nakiyah warned.

Rayna hugged her and got her clothes out of the dryer, changing back into them.

She headed out into the rain, everything she was told brewing in her brain.

Should she accept her place and learn the ways?

And what was she going to do about Matthew?

Even if he did have these so-called powers, he loved her. He cared about her. He wouldn't do that to her.

For now, things would go back to normal. Her heart belonged to him.

* * *

The next day, Nakiyah bound together the burned books and threw them in the garbage. Rayna watched as the water was cleaned from the store. Her phone kept ringing – it was Matthew's number – and she picked it up.

Nakiyah shook her head.

"Hey." Rayna greeted, smiling.

"I was wondering...do you want to go get coffee this afternoon?" Matthew asked.

"Sounds good." Rayna replied.

"All right. I'll be there at one." Matthew said

"See you then, handsome." Rayna replied with a glow.

She pressed the end call button.

"Date tonight?" Nakiyah asked, pretending not to care.

"We need to be open for Halloween." Rayna said quietly.

"We will be," Nakiyah insisted, "Power prevails...look, I must warn you. If you go through with it..."

"Nakiyah..." Rayna warned.

"Powers will mix."

"Everything will be fine. He's responsible and trustworthy."

"Says the girl who hasn't seen anything." Nakiyah warned.

"I know what I'm doing, and I'm a woman, not a girl." Rayna stated with firmness.

"It's a blood moon tonight," Nakiyah observed, "Be careful."

"Look, I just want this store to be clean and restocked on that shelf for Halloween. Let's focus on that – it's something we can agree on, and it's the biggest day of our year." Rayna distracted.

"And it will be your biggest day – if you so choose." Nakiyah reminded her.

Rayna hung her head, the decision on her shoulders like a rock. She saw bottles beginning to shake on the shelf, holding various herb waters. She closed her eyes, took a deep breath, and cleared her mind. When she looked again, the bottles were still.

"Good." Nakiyah praised, rubbing her shoulder

The bell jingled and Rose walked in.

"Here on your Saturday?" Rayna asked.

"I came to see...your aunt." Rose trailed off.

"It's okay," Nakiyah assured her, "She knows. She's one too."

"Really?" Rose asked.

"Yes," Rayna replied, "But I haven't made my decision yet."

"Rose is Earth," Nakiyah said, facing Rayna, "She's one of the corners."

"But she's so young!" Rayna exclaimed.

"She has a natural gift. Given directly from the Goddess." Nakiyah informed her.

"Who is the Goddess?" Rayna asked.

"You will learn – but she is the female counterpart to male. The ones we invoke."

"What is invoking?" Rayna asked.

"Too many questions at once – pace yourself." Nakiyah chided.

Rose took the leather-bound journal out of her backpack.

"Maybe we should read this.." Rose trailed off.

"Then...if you choose..." Nakiyah said, "Halloween will be the time – to destroy the evil ones. So you must decide soon."

Rayna and Rose looked at the book.

"I know you're seeing my dad tonight." Rose said with caution.

"How do you know?" Rayna asked.

Both Nakiyah and Rayna gazed at her.

"We lived in a small town in New Jersey before...I was bullied for being different. This blonde, thin girl who read Cosmopolitan and was passed around like a beer bottle." Rose began, "My dad confronted her parents, but they denied the whole thing. He got angry..." she trailed off.

Both their eyes widened.

"The next morning their house was being doused with water, nothing left but ashes – no survivors. They said it was faulty wiring that caused it. But I saw his eyes that night."

"They were red?" Nakiyah asked.

"Yeah. During the next week, we left our apartment with all our stuff and moved here," she paused, "I'm worried for you. I don't think he can control it."

"He won't hurt you," Nakiyah insisted, "Someone was sent to do that already."

"You know about that?" Rose asked.

"I can see things in the present and the future." Nakiyah explained to her.

"What's the future?" Rose asked.

"A battle. For our lives." Nakiyah said, choking on her words.

"Go back home," Rayna said, rubbing her back, "Read the book, and focus on something else."

"Okay," Rose conceded, "See you at Halloween?" she asked.

"I don't know." Rayna admitted.

"I hope so. Then we can be the three corners." Rose said, hugging her, "Just be careful."

Rose left the bookstore, and Nakiyah sensed more of a lightness in her but also some fear.

"Go study in the backroom," Nakiyah instructed, "I'll take care of the mess."

As Rayna headed to the backroom, she took a deep breath.

She was her own hero.

She just needed someone to stand by her side.

Chapter Eleven

Rayna sat in the cafe with Matthew, stirring her cafe mocha. She picked at her cranberry scone and ate little orts of it. Her hairline was slicked with sweat, and she wore Adidas sweatpants and a long-sleeved rayon shirt. On her feet were her running sneakers. Her face was flushed pink – partially from going two miles, partially from being there with him. Her eyelids drooped from tiredness.

Matthew wore a Bouncing Souls shirt, jeans, and Chuck Taylors. His hair was tied back in a ponytail, and his face looked slightly shaved, the goatee groomed with caution, leaving some scruff on his cheeks. His eyes blazed blue with intensity as he gazed at her.

The cafe had brick walls inside with art prints by artists like Salvador Dali, Renoir, Degas, and Van Gogh. The seats were red-cushioned and had black enamel, metal framework. The tables were checkerboard, with an attached box of chess pieces on the side.

"You seem off. What's wrong?" Matthew asked.

"Nothing. Just thinking." she murmured.

"About what?"

"About my future."

"Am I in it?" he asked, smiling.

Matthew put his hand on hers and she felt a warm heat. Rayna smiled back and clutched his hand.

"Of course," she paused, "I love you."

Matthew froze. His eyes widened. She felt intense heat go through his hand, almost a burning warmth. She closed her eyes and focused. His hand cooled.

"I haven't heard that since..." he trailed off, "Before my wife died."

Matthew paused in thought. Should he say the words? Did he mean them yet?

He looked up from the table and into her eyes, his heart beating like a tribal drum.

"I love you so much it burns inside me." Matthew whispered.

"How about we go on a wilderness walk today?" Rayna asked, "Rose could come along, and we could get some fresh air from the trees around us."

"Sounds good. Let's go get her." Matthew replied, getting up.

Rayna picked up her cup and put on the lid and took it with her.

They picked up Rose from the house, who was excited to be in contact with her element. She wore pink fleece, jeans, and hiking boots. They headed into the woods, following an uphill trail. The ground was mossy and roots extended from the ground. Some tiny white wildflowers still bloomed on the forest floor. The trees were orange, red, and yellow – like an Impressionist took a brush to the sky and added some fire to it.

Their mouths dropped. Matthew covered Rose's eyes.

There was a burned animal on a slab of granite and stones in a circle. Candles that were red and black stood between the rocks, melted down.

"Samuel." Rayna whispered.

"Who?" Matthew asked.

"Nothing. It looks like some kind of dark ritual. It's not safe here."

"Let's walk past this and over to the vista. The view will calm us down." Matthew insisted, feeling an urge in him.

They walked over to the vista of the cliff and looked at the fields and valleys, covered in the colors of the sunset. The sky was blue with a few cumulus clouds, a slight breeze in the air.

"I'm always grateful for living in Salem." Rose said, smiling.

She's a witch, a voice whispered in his ear, *They must both be destroyed.*

Tears formed in Matthew's eyes.

Killing his own daughter?

'I'm not gonna do it.' he thought.

We had a deal! The voice hissed, *Do it.*

Matthew looked at how high they were and imagined them splattering on the ground, their limbs scattered and blood dousing the rocks, their skulls burst like a watermelon dropped from a six story building.

Matthew's hands tingled.

FUCK YOU. He thought.

You're just like them. The voice whispered.

"Are you okay?" Rayna asked, touching his shoulder.

"I'm fine now. Just got distracted by my own thoughts. I was thinking about...my wife."

He remembered her engulfed in flames, laying completely still.

"Maybe we shouldn't..." Rayna trailed off.

"No. It's not that I'm hung up on her still. It's that...I don't want anything to happen to you." Matthew argued.

"Dad, she's different." Rose said, touching his hand, "She's protected."

He felt something form in his hand. He looked and saw a red rose. Rose looked at him and smiled.

"For you." Matthew whispered to Rayna, handing her the flower.

"Thank you," she said, her heart racing.

Matthew pulled her to him.

"I would do anything to keep you safe." he whispered.

"Promise?" Rayna asked.

"Let this be my promise." Matthew murmured.

He kissed her deeply, stroking her hair and cheek. She pulled away, breathless.

"Nakiyah was wrong about you," she said, "I knew it. I always did."

As they avoided the circle and walked back down through the rocky path, doubt crept into Rayna's mind.

She wondered if he could control his power and his urges.

Everything in her heart told her he would never hurt her.

Matthew walked behind Rose and Rayna. He felt his hands tingle and saw them crashing down the path, their heads bouncing off the rocks and fallen branches, bits of bone and blood dripping down the trail like a Hellish river.

Matthew clenched his fists.

This demon would not control him.

Maybe Rayna knew. If she did, she was giving him a lot of lee way. She had faith in him. And that's what he needed.

Rayna and Rose would live.

* * *

Rayna walked into *Midnight Tomes* with a smile on her face. Nakiyah raised an eyebrow.

"Did you have a good time getting coffee?" she asked.

"Yeah. And I went on a hike." Rayna replied.

"I see..." Nakiyah trailed off.

"You saw, didn't you?" Rayna accused.

"I can't control it. But the change isn't complete yet. Be cautious." she warned.

"What do you mean?" Rayna asked.

"He still has violent impulses. He controls them for the most part." Nakiyah explained, "He saw himself pushing you and Rose off the cliff. He also saw himself sending you crashing over the rocks on the trail."

"He would never do that!" Rayna exclaimed, placing her hands on her hips, "He gave me his word that he would never hurt me. He sealed it with a kiss."

"He promised his wife she'd feel no pain when she went. No one knows for sure what she felt." Nakiyah speculated.

Rayna shook her head and went to the shelves, organizing books.

The door jingled. They looked up and saw Matthew.

"I'll leave him to you." Nakiyah said, not making eye contact and walking into the back room.

"What's up?" Rayna asked, "Is it Rose?"

"No, she's fine. I forgot to ask you out for coffee and dessert tomorrow night."

"It's Sunday night. And it's a full moon." she speculated.

"Yeah, I thought maybe it would be a magical night." Matthew explained.

"I guess it would be okay..." Rayna trailed off, placing her hands firmly on the counter, grinding her teeth.

"Hey..." he said, stroking her cheek, "Are you still doubting me?"

"No...it's just...my aunt gets in my head."

"She doesn't know me as well as you do. Or as well as you will know me." Matthew said, placing his hands on hers.

"Okay," Rayna conceded, "Tomorrow night at seven."

He pulled her shoulders across the counter and kissed her deeply, his tongue exploring her mouth. She moaned and gripped his shoulders. When Matthew released her, his eyes sparked.

"You've bewitched me..." he trailed off.

Her blue eyes brightened for a second.

"You have no idea." she whispered, kissing his cheek.

He smiled and left, the bell jingling. Nakiyah walked back to the counter, pretending to count the cash in the drawer.

"Full moons are powerful," she mentioned, "They draw out our emotions like the tides."

"Are you saying....I'll be more in love with him?" Rayna asked.

"I'm saying both of your feelings will be magnified." Nakiyah explained, "And magical things can happen."

"Like what?" Rayna asked.

"It's not my right to tell you your future. I am simply explaining the present."

"Is it good or bad?" she asked.

"Could be both. Depending on both of your intentions. And that's where I'm leaving it." Nakiyah finished, "Now can you go check out our books? Halloween will be approaching. Our biggest business day of the year."

As Rayna walked to the back, she wondered what Nakiyah meant. And what Sunday had in store for her.

* * *

Kyle held tight to Rose's hand as he led her through the woods. She felt chills running down her spine and stiffening the hairs on her neck.

"It'll be fine," he chided, "It's just a bonfire with some drinking and smoking."

"I really want to go home." she pleaded, pulling away.

"I promise you – once you get there, you'll never want to leave." he said with a smile, dragging her to the center of the woods.

They came to a clearing – the same clearing from earlier in the day. The candles were lit. Men stood in the circle, of all different types. They wore jeans, flannel shirts, work boots – they all looked like blue collar guys, but they were chatting in a foreign language and drinking bottles of beer.

Rose looked around with a raised eyebrow. Kyle handed Rose a beer. She sipped it with caution.

Suddenly a bell tolled.

Flames appeared on the black and red candles, and the pile of wood logs lit in the middle of the circle. The fire reached toward the sky, The men joined hands, breaking to allow Kyle and Rose into the circle. Rose remained frozen, shivers running through her.

"It's okay," Kyle insisted, "We're all friends here."

He pulled her, and she dragged her feet towards the center.

A man entered the circle, wearing a black pinstripe suit, red tie, and he had salt and pepper hair. He smiled without showing teeth. Kyle walked like a zombie towards him, pulling Rose along.

"This is her." he said, presenting her.

"Ah. Such a lovely girl. You've made a good choice."

Samuel cupped her face and looked deep into her eyes.

"It's only right that you join us too."

"I'd rather not..." she said, backing away.

"Oh, but you're in the circle now. There's no way out. You *must* join." he said, smiling.

His eyes sparked. She inhaled the faint scent of cologne and cigarettes.

It all reminded her of her father.

Rose felt something take over her as he extended his hand.

She began to reach out – like an automaton – but a voice whispered in her ear.

It's him. Don't do it.

Rose retracted her hand with quickness.

"Samuel." she gasped.

"Oh, you know my name?" he asked, "You must've read *that* book."

His eyes became engulfed with fire, he clenched his fists. A jagged smile was on his face.

"*You* are like *her* – a witch." He turned to Kyle, "I'm sorry, my boy, but take care of it."

Kyle's eyes glowed red and he grabbed Rose, dragging her towards the bonfire. She screamed and struggled.

Rose's eyes glowed amber and a tree was uprooted and tossed on top of Samuel and Kyle, pinning them down. The other half-demons descended on her, but she raised her hands up and wooden vines entangled them, tying them to the ground.

She closed her eyes and light surrounded her.

When she opened them, she was in the bookstore, Nakiyah waiting for her.

"You've discovered your powers." she said, smiling.

Meanwhile, Samuel cast the tree into the fire. He set fire to the vines, and the other members escaped unscathed. including Kyle. Samuel shook Kyle's shoulders to focus him.

"You must finish them," he said, "Or else it's war."

"I'll do it, Master." he agreed.

Kyle's eyes glowed as he smiled.

He would get them soon.

* * *

Rayna sipped her cafe con leche while Matthew stirred cream and sugar into his black coffee.

"Dessert?" the waitress asked.

"Chocolate chip Devil's Food cake. With powdered sugar on top." he said, smiling.

"I'm up for it." Rayna said, smiling back.

As the waitress cut a piece of cake from the dessert cart, plated it, and set it in front of her, Matthew smiled faintly.

"Let me..." he whispered.

He took her fork and cut off a small piece of cake, slipping it into Rayna's mouth. He wiped a small bit of powdered sugar from her lips and licked his finger.

She moaned as she chewed the cake.

They fed each other as the night went on, fire burning in Matthew's eyes, Rayna's glowing blue.

He put money on the table.

"Let's go." he insisted.

She took his hand and he led her down a few blocks. She saw his house.

"Why are we here?" she asked.

"To continue dessert." he breathed in her ear.

"What about Rose?" Rayna asked.

"She was staying at a friend's house tonight." Matthew replied, brushing hair back from her face.

He took her hands and led her to the stairs.

"Wait...I don't know if we should..." Rayna trailed off, remembering her aunt telling her about the full moon.

He pulled her to him and looked deep in her eyes.

"Our fate is undeniable." he whispered.

He picked her up in his arms.

"You will be my queen." Matthew murmured.

"I'm 180 lbs – how are you picking me up?" she asked, breaking the mood.

He chuckled.

"Lots of gym time."

Later on as he laid her on the bed, lifted her dress, and unzipped his pants, she put her arms around his neck and wrapped her legs around his waist. He felt underneath her dress.

"No underwear...were you playing hard to get down there?" Matthew whispered.

"Just making sure," Rayna replied, "That you were him."

"Who?" he asked.

"My soulmate."

He entered her, and she felt a heat overwhelm her. As Matthew moved, Rayna moaned and clutched his shoulders, running her nails down his back. He growled and moved faster and harder.

"I want this...I want...you..." he moaned.

"You can have every inch of my body and heart." she cried out.

"I'll take it." he whispered back.

As Matthew continued to move in her, Rayna flipped him over and began riding him. She ran her hands down his chest before wrapping her hands in his hair. He was moving frantically and moaning her name.

"Come for me," she pleaded, leaning over him and kissing him.

He moaned her name into her mouth, coming, as she pulled up and screamed his name.

Something happened.

She froze.

The blue waves wound around the red heat, creating an intense electric current that melded something inside her. Rayna felt something enter her heart. She felt power rush through her, causing her to scream more. Not in pain, but in intense pleasure. He pulled her down, and clutched her to him – feeling the intense electricity flow through him.

They woke up that way, Matthew clutching Rayna's body, both of them exhaling a shuddering breath.

"What...the...fuck...was...that?" he asked, breathless.

"If I told you, you couldn't handle it." she murmured, stroking his hair.

"Tell me," he pleaded, "I want to know."

"Our powers mixed – and our souls and bodies bonded together."

Matthew sat up with suddenness.

"You know." he gasped.

"My aunt knew. She warned me this would happen, " Rayna said.

An urge came over him. He grasped her shoulders as she straddled him. An image came over him of snapping her neck. His eyes sparked.

The fire roared up in the fireplace.

"It's true..." Rayna trailed off, getting up.

"I can control it," Matthew insisted, "We're together forever now."

"There's only one way we are together forever, and that won't happen." she said, dressing.

"Why?" he asked.

"I'm a witch," Rayna paused, "And you sold your soul."

"I didn't know what I was doing!" Matthew exclaimed, getting his pants on, "All I did was shake his hand."

"And made a deal with a demon."

"I didn't kill you!" he argued, "I had opportunities, and I never did anything!"

"I'm leaving." Rayna said, going to the door.

Matthew pinned her to it.

"Let me give you something..." he pleaded, "To prove my love."

"And what's that?" she asked.

"My eternal promise," Matthew said, "I will never hurt you."

"I don't believe you." Rayna said with tears in her eyes.

"I worship you, my enchantress," he murmured, lifting her dress.

"What are you doing?" she asked, getting sparks of electricity going through her.

"Pleasuring you," he whispered, before devouring her mound.

Rayna cried out as his tongue explored inside her, flicking her clit, and stroking her walls.

It didn't take long for the electric current to burst, his name exploding on the tip of her tongue.

Matthew got back up and kissed her deeply.

"Let me take you home," he begged, "I want you to be safe."

Rayna paused, looking into his eyes.

"You want me dead. My aunt saw it."

"I swear, I don't."

"Swearing is what got you into your mess in the first place," she said.

"All I did was ask for her to go peacefully." Matthew admitted, tears filling his eyes.

"I'm not making a bargain for your life," he insisted, "I'm promising you. I can take care of my daughter, and I can take care of you too."

Rayna lowered her head, a tear trailing down.

"The only way we can be together...is if you learn our ways and become the fourth corner," she informed him, "And you won't do that, I know it."

"How do you know?" he asked.

"I -"

At that moment, Matthew pulled a pentacle necklace out of his shirt.

"Why do you think I have all these books?" he asked, holding it out to her, "I'm trying to fight what I've become."

Rayna's jaw dropped.

"Please, stay the night." Matthew whispered, pulling her against him.

He wrapped her legs around him and entered her, thrusting gently. She whimpered and buried her face in his neck.

"My beloved...My one..." he moaned, "Take all the love I have and believe it's enough."

She pulled her head back and looked into his eyes, one mirroring the other – sparking.

"Make love to me – harder." Rayna growled.

He maintained eye contact as he moved harder and faster, Rayna moaning with each thrust, her nails digging into his back and drawing blood. He groaned and moved even harder, clutching her ass and pushing her body against his as he thrust. She felt herself on edge and could barely get the words out.

"Come with me, beloved." she cried.

He thrust one last time and they screamed each others's names, bucking wildly against each other before collapsing on the rug on the floor, Matthew on top of Rayna. He kissed down her neck before kissing her with fervor.

"I would die for you." Matthew breathed.

"And I would do the same." Rayna whispered, kissing him.

* * *

Salem – 1800's

Martha kindled the fire and stirred the soup in the cauldron. A roasted chicken sat on the kitchen table on a platter. She earned enough money from fortune telling to afford this meal. A holey tablecloth was draped over the table.

She heard steps on the porch.

The door opened, and Mark walked inside.

"Dear," she greeted, kissing his cheek, "You're home!"

She hugged him tightly.

"Sit at the table," she offered, pulling out a chair, "I made a feast for you."

He sat at the table, his eyes empty. He was stiff, his hands clenched. Mark sat down and ate some of the chicken in silence, sipping the soup.

"I'm so glad to have you home." Martha said, tears in her eyes.

"You tell fortunes and knit and tend to the wounded. But you have no idea what they saw – what I saw." Mark began.

"I saw you would come home. I knew you were safe." she argued.

"In every letter, you detailed home life – only making me wish I was there, instead of on the battlefield, watching men get shot and stabbed with bayonets and swords. You were here, eating peaceful meals, playing with our children, while I ate whatever scraps we were able to get." Mark continued.

"I thought of you every second of every day! I prayed to the Goddess that my vision wasn't just wishes." Martha said, standing up from the table.

Mark stood up, his eyes glowing red.

"I saw bloodshed – murder – cannonballs destroying houses and killing innocent people – I survived a bullet to the shoulder. And you say, "I made a feast for you'," he said, his heart like granite, "And expect it will make up for all of the carnage I saw.".

"Darling, I never meant to belittle what happened to you," she insisted, trying to kiss him.

"Get away, witch!" he exclaimed, pushing her against the wall.

Martha's head hit hard, and she slumped to the floor.

Mark ran upstairs and looked for their daughter but she was nowhere to be found.

He came back downstairs and looked at the fireplace. The flames reflected themselves in his eyes.. The fire shot up from the hearth and caught on the ceiling and walls.

Mark looked and saw Martha's eyes open.

"If I die, you die too." she moaned.

He heard the door lock from the outside.

Mark tried to break through the windows, but they wouldn't break.

"Hag! You commit murder!" he accused.

"So do you..." Martha trailed off.

"Til death do us part." she finished.

The house was engulfed in flames and their screams echoed into the farmland.

The next morning, bare frames of the house remained.

Mark's skeleton was splayed on the floor. Martha's was beside him, the bony arms wrapped around his waist.

Til death do them part indeed.

Chapter Twelve

Rayna woke up in his arms, her back to his. She stirred, trying to move her arm which fell asleep. She felt him reaching around and rubbing it.

"Rose will be home in a few hours." Rayna reminded him.

"So we have a few hours..." Matthew said, kissing her neck.

"Hm, what can we do with a few hours?" she asked turning him over, and sliding down his legs.

"What are you doing?" he asked.

"Returning the favor." Rayna replied, her blue eyes sparking red.

As she took him in her mouth, it began to rain outside. Matthew moaned with every movement, massaging her head.

As he climaxed, a downpour started outside and the fire inside the hearth raised towards the flue.

Rayna gazed at him, shaking.

"Why are you trembling?" Matthew asked.

"I'm afraid of you." she admitted.

"You're mine forever," he whispered, "The cycle is broken."

"My mother was married, and she died in a house fire – with my father." Rayna told him.

He wrapped his fingers in her hair and kissed her.

"I'm not your father," Matthew whispered, "I'm not Samuel, I'm not anyone else..."

He paused.

"I'm Matthew Johansen, inventory expert....and the fourth corner. I pledged that to you. Remember ?"

"Unfortunately." Rayna admitted.

"You regret it?" he asked in shock.

"I'm worried." she clarified and then paused.

Rayna got a chill up her back.

"Something's wrong." she gasped.

"What?"

"Rose." Rayna spoke, putting on her clothes.

"What happened??" Matthew asked, throwing on his as well.

"He found her."

"Jesus." he muttered, both of them running to his car.

They hoped they weren't too late.

* * *

Kyle stood outside the cafe, staring with red flamed eyes.. Rose was reading the leather-bound book, ignoring the world outside.

"Rose..."

Her eyes went wide. She backed up against the wall.

"Go away!" Rose yelled.

"Not gonna happen..." Kyle sang.

"Lock the door!" she yelled.

The owner came to the front door.

"It's just your boyfriend." she said, opening the door.

As the owner stood in the doorframe, a fireball hit her. She burned, screaming, until there was nothing left.

"You chose your fate. So did your father." Kyle hissed.

He aimed a fireball at her, but Rose dodged it and hid behind the counter.

Kyle sent another one into the coffee machine, splattering burning hot coffee all over her.

Rose screamed.

Rayna's car screeched to a halt in front of the cafe, both of them rushing out.

"The extermination stops here." Matthew growled, his eyes red, sparking blue.

Rayna looked and saw Rose behind the counter, her arms covered in burns.

"Just try -" he began.

Kyle didn't finish his sentence. A fireball hit him, engulfing him in flames. Animal like whines and screams came from his body.

But then Kyle reappeared – flames surrounding him.

"Idiot. Taking in fire only makes me stronger." he growled.

Kyle held his hands above his head and formed a huge fireball. Rayna and Matthew dove behind the counter and covered Rose. The fireball hit the cafe, the place ablaze. They began to choke on smoke. Rayna aimed her hands at the walls and shot a stream of water at the flames.

But nothing happened.

Kyle laughed and walked away.

"Rest in ashes, heathens." he chuckled, walking away.

"What do we do?!" Rayna asked.

Matthew looked at her, his eyes sparking. Her eyes sparked, too. They nodded at each other.

"We can do this." Rayna said with a steadiness in her voice.

They aimed their hands towards each other and shot out a red & blue stream of light at the walls and roof. The flames slowly disappeared until they were completely gone.

"It...hurts..." Rose whimpered, looking at her arms.

Rayna held her hands over her arms. Rose felt a cooling sensation, the pain receding.

"Nakiyah can heal you." Rayna advised, "She knows the ways."

"Is she gonna stick pins into a doll of me?" Matthew asked.

"She's not into voodoo – and I think she will sense the difference in you." Rayna replied.

"Grab the book and you two can stay with me. Samuel will know we aren't dead." Rayna ordered.

They got in Rayna's car and drove to Nakiyah's apartment.

Nakiyah would be able to discern what was ahead and leave no trace of burns on Rose.

Rayna only hoped she didn't take aim at Matthew.

He started to prove he could change.

* * *

Nakiyah watched her apartment door with expectancy. Sure enough, Rayna opened it and entered with Matthew and Rose.

"So...the bond has happened." Nakiyah concluded.

"How did you know?" Matthew asked.

"Your eyes aren't just glowing red anymore."

"We noticed that ourselves." Rayna agreed, "Is this...part of it?"

"It means he has broken free, and you two are soulmates," Nakiyah paused, "You are strong enough to get the demon out of you. You just retained the powers because of your corner."

"What is this power Rayna and I have now?" he asked.

"It is double the intensity – double the strength. It is a form of magic more powerful than most." she began, "With this, we may have a fighting chance."

"We brought Rose to you..." Rayna trailed off, showing her Rose's arms.

"The coffee." Nakiyah said, her vision giving her the answers.

"Can you heal it?" Rose asked, her voice weak with pain.

"Yes, I can." Nakiyah replied.

She went into the kitchen and put a kettle on, mixing various herbs in a tea ball and placing it in a mug.

"Tea?" Rose asked.

"The herbs on your skin would hurt too much. It works better if it's ingested." Nakiyah replied.

She lit a tall candle in a glass jar with strange writing on it.

"What is that?" Rayna asked.

"A protection candle. As long as this is lit, we're safe here." Nakiyah replied, "Kyle thinks you're dead, but Samuel will know you're not."

Nakiyah placed her hands on Rayna's shoulders.

"You have to avenge your ancestry," she told her, "You have to fight. For Tituba."

The kettle whistled. Nakiyah poured the water into the mug and brought it to the table.

"Let it steep for a few minutes, then sip it. I promise you it's not gross." she said with a faint smile.

Rose inhaled the steam from the mug. It smelled fragrant and sweet. Tears came to her eyes.

"It smells like my mom's perfume." she choked out.

"Dear, you will always miss your mother," Nakiyah said with softness, "But don't let grief deter you. Use your sadness and anger as fuel."

As she relived the night with Kyle, her eyes glowed amber.

"He almost burned me alive." she growled.

"Yes, he did. Drink this tea, and then go home and rest. You two as well – seeing the active night you two had, which has scarred me for a while." Nakiyah joked.

"You're the one with the clairvoyance." Rayna reminded her, smirking.

"And at times, I regret it." Nakiyah said, smiling faintly.

"You can stay with us." Matthew said, taking Rayna's hand.

Rose drank the last of the tea and put the mug down.

"Thank you, Nakiyah." Rose said.

"Call me auntie. We're family now." she replied smiling.

"Ok...auntie." Rose said, hugging her.

Nakiyah hugged her back, tears starting to fill her eyes as she saw what they faced.

Rayna and Matthew sent a stream of energy at Samuel, weakening him, making him frail and aged. But Kyle threw a fireball at Matthew. He screamed and fell to the ground. Rayna quickly sent a stream of water at him, putting out the fire. She leaned down by him.

"Talk to me..." she pleaded, placing a hand on his heart.

His heartbeat grew weaker.

Tears filled her eyes.

"The battle will be hard fought. But we have to be prepared for anything. Kyle is a clever one." Nakiyah said.

"Can he harm us at our house?" Rose asked.

"No, not if you light these protection candles." Nakiyah replied, handing them two tall candles.

"We will use them well." Rayna said, hugging her.

"I will put a circle of protection around your place as strong as I can." Nakiyah added.

"Thank you." Matthew murmured.

Nakiyah eyed him like a scorpion. She turned her back as they left.

As he closed the door, Nakiyah let out a deep breath and let herself cry.

She wasn't sure they could fight fate.

Samuel wanted them all dead – and he could get what he wanted.

Chapter Thirteen

Salem – July 4, 1921

Betty was sipping a gin & tonic and leaning on the bar in the speakeasy. She took an inhale from a cigarette and blew out the smoke in a swirl. From across the room, she saw a man with chestnut hair and blue eyes in a beige suit. She smiled and took a bottle of pink water out of her purse, dabbed it on her ears and neck, and put it back in the purse. She watched people dance and drink and waited. Sure enough, he walked over to the bar.

"Can I buy you a drink?" he asked.

"You can refill mine." she said, smirking.

He ordered her another gin & tonic and a martini for himself.

"What's your name?" he asked.

"Betty. Yours?" she asked.

"Richard. What do you do?" he asked.

"I'm a dancer." she explained.

"Wow. That takes a bit of a spitfire." he replied.

"That it does." she said, sipping her drink.

He sipped his martini and slowly moved his hand over to hers, touching her fingers. She looked down and stroked his fingers with hers. She saw him shiver.

"What do you do?" Betty asked in a low voice.

"I work for a magazine."

"Well off." she commented.

"I make enough to live this lifestyle." Richard said, smiling.

"Me too." she said, smiling, "My performances draw in...the gentlemen."

"Shall we dance?" he asked.

"Sure."

They went to the dance floor and danced the Charleston, Richard feeling heat flow through him, Betty feeling emotions and warmth overcome her. The music slowed, and he pulled her to him, going into a waltz. As he dipped her, he pressed into her, and she felt his hardness against her.

"There's an empty stock room in the back." Betty breathed.

He let go of her, and she went into the back. He waited a few minutes and followed. Betty pushed him against the wall, kissing him with fervor, unbuttoning his shirt and running her fingers across his six-pack abs. He gasped and unbuttoned her dress, revealing a black lace bustier with lace threaded through eyelets.

"What's underneath?" Richard whispered.

"Only one way to find out." Betty replied.

She untied the laces, and slowly opened the bustier, revealing her ample breasts and thick curves. He glanced at her panties – black satin with lace trim.

"Ooh, I can't leave this laying on the floor." Betty murmured, bending over and picking it up, running her hands up her legs.

He grabbed her ass and pulled it towards him, pressing his hardness against her cheeks.

"Sorry, I'm not like those cheap whores." Betty said, standing up.

"No, you're not," he breathed, "But what are you?"

"I'm a simple girl with a bewitching touch." Betty whispered, licking her way down his chest to his abdomen.

"Seems you forgot something..." he trailed off, unbuttoning his pants.

"You're right." she replied, releasing his length and taking it in her mouth, getting on her knees.

She ran her tongue up and down it, keeping rapid, tight movements as Richard entangled his fingers in her hair. Just as she felt his hands tightened, she pulled away.

"What the -" Richard began.

"I want to come as bad as you do." Betty said, sliding down her panties.

"You are so smoking hot." he growled.

"Make me wet." she ordered, pulling her to him.

Richard thrusted into her hard and fast, her leg over his shoulder. Betty clutched him, leaning against his shoulder to muffle her moans. She felt his fire enter her, sending electricity through her. He gasped as he felt an invigorating energy flow through him. As they climaxed, they felt an electric current flow through both of them, both of them crying out the other's name.

Betty lowered her leg and slumped against him, Richard leaning against a wall, breathing hard.

"Jesus Christ, what was that?" he asked.

"I know what you are." she breathed.

"What?" Richard asked, surprised.

"And you know what I am." Betty said, looking him in the eyes, hers glowing green.

"So..." he trailed off.

"We're meant to be." she whispered, her mouth inches from his ear.

Richard threaded his hand in her hair.

"You're...the one I've been waiting for?" he asked.

"Yes. And I've been waiting for you, too."

He kissed her deeply, exploring her mouth and clutching her to him. Betty moaned into his mouth and pulled away.

"He'll be looking for us." Betty commented.

"Yes," Richard agreed, "He'll know."

"I don't know if we can fight him..." she trailed off.

"We can try. We can always try." he encouraged, "But let's make the most of the moment."

The next day, they went to a Justice of the Peace.

They would fight him when the time came.

* * *

Matthew opened the door of his house and let Rose and Rayna in. Rayna placed the candles on the coffee table and lit them.

"Do you think it'll work?" Rose asked.

"Magick is powerful. Nakiyah charged these candles with her power. We're safe here." Rayna replied, stroking Rose's hair.

"I'll put some coffee on," Matthew said.

"Ooh fancy." Rayna said with a smile.

"I can make you a cappuccino. Nothing fancy, but I can add allspice and cinnamon."

"Sounds delicious." Rayna replied, taking a seat on the couch next to Rose.

Together, they opened the leather-bound book.

"I found something Nakiyah mentioned today..." Rose trailed off.

"What?"

"You know how she said your powers combined?" Rose asked.

"Yeah..." Rayna trailed off.

Rose flipped through the book to the middle. She pointed at the date.

July 4, 1920.

Rayna read through the entry, her eyes widening She turned page after page, shivering as she continued reading. There was one last paragraph, ten pages later...

"We are headed to the circle. Hopefully our powers can redeem my ancestors and break the cycle. I fear he is too powerful – he has had centuries to grow stronger through the deaths he caused. My beloved is beckoning to me...may future generations read this and find the strength to stop him if we don't."

Matthew came in the room and saw Rayna's tears. He immediately kneeled down by her and put the coffee on the table.

"What's wrong?" he asked.

"Nothing and everything. My ancestors...their powers bonded with their beloveds. But...they couldn't defeat him." Rayna stammered.

"Let me see..." Matthew said, taking the open book and flipping back.

After reading the pages, he looked deep into her eyes.

"We *are* strong enough. We have the four corners. We're using everything we have." Matthew said, cupping her face, "I will not let him hurt you."

Rayna kissed him gently and hugged him.

"Maybe we can." she said with hesitance.

"No, we CAN." Matthew said, grasping her shoulders.

The electricity in his eyes lit up hers.

"We can." she said with hardness like a boulder.

They joined hands – Rayna, Matthew, and Rose – and their eyes glowed.

They were ready to fight.

* * *

Rayna entered the bookstore the next day, looking tired and worn out. Nakiyah looked up from the inventory list for the box in front of her and gave her a look with soft eyes.

"Practicing?" she asked.

"One battle and we were drained. We had to." Rayna said, sitting behind the counter and leaning her head on it.

"Rose!" Nakiyah called.

Rayna looked up and saw Rose – wearing a name tag and a t-shirt with the store's emblem on it.

"She's working here now?" Rayna asked.

"She has her working papers. She's 18," she paused and turned to Rose, "Go to the cafe and get Rayna two coffees – one dark roast, light and sweet – and a pumpkin spice latte with two extra shots of espresso & six sweeteners. Get me an apple cider. And get yourself whatever you want. Oh, and three scones – blueberry for Rayna, cinnamon for me, and whichever one you want."

"I kinda like cranberry." Rose admitted.

"A bit early for Christmas, sweetie." Rayna said.

"It's never too early for Christmas, though Halloween is just around the corner. The stores will be switching decorations soon and stocking up on ornaments, fake trees, and tinsel." Nakiyah reminded her.

"Do they have peppermint mocha lattes available yet?!" Rose asked excitedly.

"Not until after Halloween, but I can make you one." Rayna said, "When we get home, I'll doctor up one."

"Thanks Rayna. I think I'll just get a mocha cappuccino in the meantime." Rose replied with gratitude.

"At least you get the mocha." Nakiyah said, handing her a twenty and a ten.

"Thanks auntie!" Rose said, running down the street.

"Don't run on the way back!" Rayna shouted, hoping she heard.

"She's 18. And she's at the top of her class." Nakiyah said, picking up Rayna's head, "Come on, your caffeine will be here soon."

Rayna looked through the box, holding up each item as Nakiyah checked it off. They had a smooth method running. Nakiyah slid a book over to her.

"Candle magic?" Rayna asked.

"It will help. Just follow the rituals and spells." Nakiyah replied, stroking her hair.

"Don't you need this?" she asked.

"I've been preparing for this for years. I've practiced – I've honed my spell casting skills – I've kept with the rituals and celebrations. I've got my altar just the way I want it -"

"Altar?" Rayna asked.

"Yes, you have to have a space for your work and your altar. It explains it in one of the books I gave you!" Nakiyah slapped her shoulder lightly, "Girl, read!"

"I've had so much going on the past few weeks. No reading time." Rayna said, yawning.

"Well, then, I'm giving you two days off just to read. You *need* this knowledge to survive and to avenge your ancestors." Nakiyah said.

Rose came in with the drinks and scones. She placed Rayna's two coffees in front of her with her scone and did the same for Nakiyah. She herself stood at the counter and sipped her cappuccino. Rayna practically gulped down the dark roast coffee, barely stopping for a breath.

I have to go look at our financials." Nakiyah said, walking into the back.

"Help me check off this inventory." Rayna said, kissing her forehead.

Rose picked up the items, and Rayna checked them off. Rayna remembered Nakiyah teaching her at that age.

The ritual – even of inventory – continued, the elders teaching the young ones.

Rayna just hoped she could help Rose prepare for what was coming.

* * *

The door shut with a thud as Rayna collapsed on the couch. Matthew was already sitting in the armchair, rubbing his eyes.

"How was work?" he asked, yawning.

"Fine," Rayna paused, "Look, Matthew, I was wondering – what if we practiced what we talk about and forgive Samuel?"

Matthew's head almost flipped around, his eyes sparking blue and red.

"Calm down..." Rayna chided, reaching out for his hand.

He pulled it away.

"I just believe that love and kindness will fix what's wrong!" Rayna yelled back.

"Forgiveness?! He killed my wife and your ancestors!" He yelled.

The fire in the fireplace roared.

He took a deep breath and it calmed.

"You are so childish and naïve." he muttered.

"I am not. I'm just an optimist, and I believe in love. Don't you?" she asked with weakness.

"I did." he said, dropping off.

"You don't love me?" she asked with tears in her eyes.

"I don't know if I can have someone who's a child herself raising my kid."

He shut his eyes as soon as the words came out.

"Rayna, I didn't mean that -" Matthew started.

"Yes, you did. You meant exactly that." Rayna said with a shaky voice. "We're bonded for life. I'll fight with you, but...as for us...I don't know. If there's a way to break it, I'll find out...tonight."

"Don't do this." he pleaded.

"I thought you were the one. I thought you understood me better than anyone." Rayna said, looking down, "Looks like my judgment is as flawed as me being childish and naïve."

Rose walked down the stairs.

"What's going on?" she asked, dressed in her warm pajamas.

"I'm sorry, sweetie. But I have to leave." Rayna said, choking up.

"No! You can't leave! He'll find you!" Rose argued, wrapping her arms around Rayna.

"I'd go to Nakiyah's, but she's still mad at me." she replied, "I have to head home."

"No, you don't." a voice said.

She looked up and saw Nakiyah in the doorway.

"I'm not mad at you. I just wish you understood. That won't stop me from protecting you. Come on, I'll get your clothes." Nakiyah said.

As Rayna and Nakiyah went into their bedroom and packed, Nakiyah shook her head.

"I told you not to trust him." she chided.

"He insulted me. He said I'm not fit to mother his kid." Rayna argued.

"He was angry. Just be glad he didn't burn you alive."

"So you think the tendency is still there?" Rayna asked.

"No, I don't. He controlled his temper to a degree. He's learned his lesson. Now you have to learn yours." Nakiyah finished.

"And what's that?" Rayna asked.

"If you find out how to undo this...you will lose him forever. Do you really want that?" Nakiyah asked.

Tears filled Rayna's eyes and slid down her cheeks. Nakiyah hugged her close.

"Just take a one day breather. You'll be safe at my place."

Rayna and Nakiyah walked downstairs with an overnight bag. Matthew eyes were wet, as were Rose's.

"Think about what you want," Rayna whispered, "I'll do the same."

"I want YOU."

"Didn't sound like it a few minutes ago. I think we really need some breathing space."

"I let my temper get the best of me." he argued.

"Then work on that for a day." Rayna said with harshness, walking out the door with Nakiyah and closing it.

"Don't lose her, Dad." Rose pleaded.

"I'm not going to. I'll do whatever it takes to get her back." he said with a broken voice.

They sat on the couch, Rose clutching her dad, Matthew staring into the fire, looking for answers.

* * *

Nakiyah made Rayna a cup of lavender tea. They both sat in the living room with Amy Winehouse playing on the stereo. They sipped their drinks and sat in silence.

"He didn't mean it." Nakiyah said with simplicity.

"Part of me knows he didn't. But part of me thinks...he feels it inside." Rayna replied, tucking her legs under her.

"He doesn't. I can see, remember?" Nakiyah reminded her.

"What is this doing to Rose?" Rayna asked, holding her head.

"It's...not having a good effect on her."

"Don't bullshit me. How is it affecting her?" Rayna demanded.

"She's very upset. I see her crying in her room and holding the bunny her mother made for her."

"At 18?"

Nakiyah stared at her.

"Yet you're clutching a quilt your mother made as if you were adrift on the sea and needed warmth and a reminder of her love." Nakiyah observed.

"It's just a reminder. The dead can't be with us." Rayna murmured, a tear slipping down her face.

The song they were listening to started skipping.

I told you I'm no good...I told you I'm no good...I told you I'm no good...

Nakiyah jumped up spilling her tea.

"What's wrong?" Rayna asked.

A window shattered and a face appeared. A face with a jagged smile, salt and pepper hair, and red eyes.

"Be gone!" Nakiyah yelled, "This is consecrated space!"

"Oh, I'll still get you. I always get what I want." the face said with a smile.

"Samuel..." Rayna choked out.

"I can shake you up more than this." he mused.

The walls shook with violence and the floorboards shifted. Nakiyah held onto the banister of the staircase. Rayna clutched the couch as she screamed.

"You can't touch us!" Nakiyah yelled.

"Who says I have to touch you?" he asked.

He held his hands above his head and closed his eyes. A fireball started to amass.

"Momma….Momma…Momma…Momma…Momma…"   Rayna choked out, clutching the quilt.

A light splintered into the living room, causing a bright shining luminescence. Rayna and Nakiyah shielded their eyes. When it disappeared, they looked and saw Rayna's mother in a wispy form.

"Momma…" she called.

"Baby, I'll protect you. Nakiyah, keep holding onto the banister. This will be intense." she said in an angelic tone.

She aimed her hands at Samuel and shot a huge burst of light at him. He screamed and it sent him flying acres and acres away.

"You fucking bitch!" his scream echoed.

The house jumped off the ground and landed with the power. Rayna was breathing heavy and hard, her hyperventilation getting worse.

"Sister…" Nakiyah said, running over to Rayna.

Rayna's mother glided over to her. She placed her hand on Rayna's heart, and her heartbeat slowed – her breathing returned to normal increment by increment.

"Thank you, Momma." she whispered.

She hugged her ghostly form which had a surprising solidness to it. She smelled her perfume – roses, bergamot, and sandalwood.

"I have to go." her mother said, releasing her.

"Will I ever see you again?" Rayna asked.

She smiled at Rayna.

"I love you. Forever."

She evaporated into the air, and tears came to Rayna's eyes.

"The dead are always with us," Nakiyah said, "You just had to discover it for yourself."

"We need to get to Matthew and Rose." Rayna commanded, grabbing her overnight bag.

"We're not safe traveling on foot." Nakiyah said, "He'll be looking for us."

"How the hell else can we get there?" Rayna asked.

"Close your eyes with me. And just visualize the living room." Nakiyah said.

Rayna closed her eyes and saw the fireplace – the comfy couch – the crocheted afghan. When she opened them again, they were standing right there.

"How the..." she began.

"You've learned light travel." Nakiyah said, smiling.

"How did you two get here?" Matthew asked, coming in from the kitchen.

"You'll find out. But for now, we have bigger issues at hand." Nakiyah replied.

"Samuel?" he asked.

"He attacked Nakiyah's house." Rayna said, still shaking.

"How did you two survive?" he asked.

"My mother." Rayna murmured.

"What?" he asked, eyes wide.

"Sit. It's a long story." Nakiyah said.

Matthew and Rayna sat in the couch and Nakiyah sat in the armchair as they told him the tale of their experience. His eyes sparked with anger, his mouth was agape with shock.

"Nowhere is safe." Rayna said.

"I shouldn't be shocked by any of this...it's been like watching Hocus Pocus on repeat for the past few weeks...but it means we have to be on our defenses at all times." he said once they were finished.

"Hell has come to Earth," Nakiyah observed, "And we must defend our town against it."

"Hell. I'd expect nothing less." Matthew muttered.

* * *

It was 5AM. Matthew was up til 2 talking with Nakiyah and Rayna. They both conked out in the living room. He made coffee, got dressed, and headed to work. He was walking up to the store when he felt a tap on the shoulder.

"Excuse me, sir, I have these burns all over my chest, and I'm looking for something to heal them." the man asked.

Matthew turned around and saw a man in a flannel shirt, jeans, and work boots with an 'America' hat on his head.

"You don't look like someone who would go to our store." Matthew commented.

"Yeah...well...just because you're blue collar doesn't mean you're an asshole."

"I don't have anything, but..." he cut himself off.

The man had red sparks in his eyes. Matthew felt a magnetic pull to him.

"Red Chapman. Nice to meet you." the man said.

He held out his hand.

Matthew started to extend his to shake it, but he snapped out of it and pulled it away.

"I know who you are." Matthew growled.

The facade faded and Samuel appeared in his usual attire.

"You're not stupid like you were. Just makes things harder on yourself." he said with a sinister smile.

Matthew immediately aimed his hands at him and a bolt of red energy shot out, sending Samuel crashing into Matthew's car, his arms bending in strange directions, his leg snapping. Samuel opened his eyes, and they glowed red.

"Fool." he husked.

He snapped his leg back together and bent his arms into their usual shape.

"You think you can break me, mortal?!" he boomed.

He held his hands out and formed fire in a flash, aiming it at Matthew, but Matthew was ready. He shot out another wave of red energy at the fire, extinguishing it. His eyes sparked red and blue. Samuel gritted his teeth.

"So...you've bonded. I've dealt with ones like you before, and they failed, too. You, your true love, and your daughter will all perish by our hands.You will all end up ghosts, doomed to wander the earth with no home and no respite from the pain."

Samuel disappeared in a poof of flame. Matthew was out of breath from the expenditure of power. He dialed the main office and left a message.

"I'm taking a sick day. I have the flu." he said, hanging up with immediacy.

Matthew yanked his dented door open, slamming it shut and speeding home.

He had to warn them. The battle was upon them. Soon.

Chapter Fourteen

Salem – 1930

Betty and Richard walked to the circle, hand in hand, broken out in a cold sweat. They needed to break the cycle. They left their daughter with Betty's mother and made sure to give her the book to hide.

Red and black candles were lit around the circle of rocks. Samuel appeared in a puff of fire.

Betty's hatred coursed through her like ocean waves. Her eyes sparked red and blue. So did Richard's. Samuel smirked.

"Bonded. No matter...it will not save you." he murmured.

He held up his hands and held out a fireball. He shot it at them, but they aimed both their hands at it with lightning speed and sent streaks of blue and red energy at it, extinguishing it. Then they struck Samuel with it. He writhed in pain and screamed.

Men started to surround them inside the confines of the circle. Breaking their concentration, the streams of energy stopped. The men all held their hands above their heads, chanting, and forming fireballs in their hands. Samuel moved to the center of the circle where they were.

"Fools. I want you to relish your impending deaths." he said, smiling his toothy smile.

Betty clutched Richard.

"We failed." she cried, tears streaking her face.

"Nothing will part us. Not in this life, not in the next. I am yours. Forever."

"I am yours too, my beloved." she whispered.

He kissed her deeply just as the nine fireballs hit them. They whined in scorching pain as the flames engulfed them, burning them to nothing. No trace was left.

Samuel grinned, but stopped.

There were more.

"Cursed beings keep birthing more heathens. I will finish the job. No matter how long it takes." he growled.

The men nodded.

"My hoard of demons will be undefeatable."

Everyone smiled.

* * *

Rayna bolted up from the bed, her cami drenched in sweat, her breathing laboured. Matthew sat up and put his arm around her.

"What's wrong?" he asked.

"I – I – I saw them die." she choked out.

"Who?" he asked.

"My ancestors. The bonded ones. They died. Everyone in the circle killed them. Samuel he – he – he drew it out just to torture them." she sobbed.

Matthew held her close to him and stroked her hair.

"Look, we're gonna do everything we can to end this bullshit." he insisted, " We're going to do finish the job they started."

He lifted her chin so she was looking in his eyes.

"Your ancestors will be avenged. I'm not gonna let this asshole go unpunished." Matthew said, kissing her.

She let her tongue explore his mouth and he drew Rayna down to the mattress, stroking her sides, and running his hand along her thighs.

"Matthew..." she moaned, as he stroked her sensitive spot.

"Let me help you forget.." he crooned, kissing down her neck and sucking on her breasts.

She arched against him and cried out, once again feeling the electricity spark through her. She felt her soul stretch itself out in her body, radiating light from her form.

There was a knock at the door.

"Can you two keep it down?" Rose asked.

"Sorry, sweetie." Matthew said, blushing.

He heard her footsteps go back into her room, the door closing.

"Isn't it wrong that she knows?" Rayna asked.

"She's eighteen. I don't want to know what *she* was doing before Kyle." he scoffed.

"True. They get sex education around this time." Rayna agreed.

"Thanks. So comforting." he quipped.

"Let her grow on her own. Granted, Kyle wasn't a good choice – but she was rebelling." Rayna commented.

"I have to say," Matthew agreed, "You've been a good influence on her."

"When you have positive people around you, good things happen." Rayna told him.

"Let's try to go back to sleep," Matthew said, "It's four in the morning, and I go in at six."

"Yeah, I go in at nine." Rayna agreed.

They spooned, Matthew's arms around her waist, and Rayna snuggled into him. She drifted off, feeling safer in her lover's arms.

* * *

That morning, Rayna poured herself a cup of dark roast, adding cream and sweetener. She whipped up some scrambled eggs for the three of them with shredded white cheddar on top, along with English muffins with strawberry jam. She fried up some bacon and drained it on a paper towel. She made it extra crispy, like her mother did.

"Breakfast!" Rayna called as she fixed Matthew's coffee and set aside a latte for Rose.

They both came down the stairs, Matthew in a white button down shirt and gray slacks, Rose in a pink peasant top and khaki dress pants with pink ballet flats. Her dirty blonde hair was curled, cascading down her shoulders.

"Looking good for someone today?" Rayna asked.

"No, just doing it for myself." Rose said, sitting down at the breakfast nook.

"That's always a good reason." Matthew said, with a little too much enthusiasm.

Rayna cleared her throat, eyeing Matthew.

"Um...so...got a date for the Halloween dance yet?" he asked Rose.

"No. I don't think I'll go." Rose said, with a gloomy look in her eyes.

Rayna shrugged.

"Who knows? Maybe you'll find a date." she commented.

"Yeah...uh...maybe you'll find...the right guy..." Matthew stammered.

Rose took a last bite of bacon and swallowed the rest of her latte.

"Yeah, right." she said, rolling her eyes, "I gotta go."

"Be careful out there!" Matthew warned, "It's daytime!"

"I know...no magic in daytime." she agreed.

As the door closed behind her, Rayna shook her head.

"Took one bite of her eggs, ate one piece of bacon, one bite of the muffin..." she trailed off, "All she finished was the coffee."

"Something's up." Matthew agreed.

"You know teenagers...they keep their life in the dark."

"Were you like that?" he asked with a smirk.

"Wouldn't you like to know?" Rayna joked, smiling.

* * *

Nakiyah wrapped up a large quartz crystal for a customer that reflected the sunlight outside. She smiled as she felt the power within it. She looked at the woman in front of her. Her intuition told her that she was meek and the bruise on her shoulder told her she was in a bad situation.

"You know...I have something that's meant for you," Nakiyah said, going into the cabinet, and taking out a bracelet made of gemstones, "This is for protection."

"Oh, I don't need protection." the woman lied, giving a weak smile. "Just try it out."

"...thanks..." the woman said awkwardly, slipping on the bracelet.

Rayna walked up from the back as the woman exited.

"Abused?" she asked.

"How did you -"

"I heard what you said and made my own conclusions."

"She will be fine. I can see it." Nakiyah said, sipping her green tea.

"I need a coffee, so I'm gonna run to the cafe down the street." Rayna said, grabbing her handbag.

"Okay. Be careful." Nakiyah warned.

Rayna strolled down the avenue, admiring the fall foliage that splattered the streets with orange, red, and yellow leaves. She went into the cafe and got in line, not shocked by the lunch break rush. As she walked to the cashier and gave her the order for her drink, a hand tapped her on the shoulder. She turned and saw a man with hair in a ponytail, goatee, and golden eyes.

"Here, let me pay for your coffee," he offered, "My name is John Trent."

He offered her his hand.

Rayna started to reach out, but she looked in his eyes. They sparked red.

She pulled him by the collar, his ear close to her mouth.

"I'm not a dumb bitch. If you want to start something, you'll be deeply sorry. I have more than enough power to make you fly across the state like my mother did. Just try me." she growled.

He sneered at her.

"Well, don't say I didn't offer." he smiled, putting his facade back on.

Samuel stormed outside the cafe and, once he was in the alley, he changed appearance.

"That fucking whore. I'll kill her if it's the last thing I ever do. Her and that righteous aunt."

Samuel disappeared in a puff of smoke.

Back in the cafe, Rayna paid for her coffee.

"Are you crazy? He was a cute guy! And you could've gotten coffee for nothing!" the cashier marveled.

"Things aren't always what they appear," Rayna said, half-smiling, "And I already have a cute guy." she added, winking.

The cashier giggled and handed her the drink.

Rayna strolled back to the bookstore, confident. Strong.

He'd be sorry he ever crossed her path.

* * *

Salem – 1944

Patricia sipped a bottle of coke as she dipped her hips back and forth at a dance filled with military men and single women. A server placed a plate of chili cheese fries in front of her. As she picked at them, she looked up and saw a man staring at her from across the room. He had brown eyes and dark brown hair, in a military uniform. He walked over and sat down next to her.

"What's your name, doll?" he asked.

"Patricia. Yours?" she asked.

"William. Having a good time?" he asked.

"Yeah," she admitted, "My parents don't know I snuck out. They would never let me go to a dance like this."

"What do you do?" he asked.

"I'm a seamstress at my mom's dress store." Patricia admitted.

"Would you like to dance?" he asked.

"Sure." she agreed.

He whipped her around the dance floor as the band played. When the music slowed down, they were sweaty with the expenditure of energy.They went back to the table and ordered two more Cokes.

"So what are you doing here?" Patricia asked.

"I'm a single guy on the lookout for the right woman." William said, smirking.

"My mother says I'm too outspoken and fiery. That guys don't like that." she admitted.

William ran a hand through her chocolate hair, then stroked her caramel toned cheek.

"I prefer a woman with a backbone. Someone who can hold her end of a debate and also take care of the house. Balance is key." he said.

"You've never had a meal like I've cooked." Patricia said, smiling.

"How about I stop by the shop this week when you're closing? I can take you home, and we can have a late supper." he suggested.

"That would be nice...do you need the address?" she asked.

"It's Salem...I don't think there are a lot of dressmakers." he said, grinning.

Patricia looked at her watch.

"Shoot! It's midnight. I gotta sneak back home." she said, jumping up.

William got up and grabbed her hand, pulling her to him, and kissing her passionately. She melted against him, putting her arms around his neck.

As William broke away, he let out a breath.

"Damn. You're quite a woman." he whispered.

She grinned.

"You have no idea."

As Patricia took a taxi back to her grandmother's house and climbed up the lattice to her bedroom window, she smiled.

She just hoped this week on leave wasn't the last she'd be seeing him.

* * *

"Rayna!" Nakiyah called.

Rayna closed the leather-bound book and looked up.

"These women need help finding books." she told Rayna.

Rayna led them to the stacks, listening to the titles and taking them off the shelves. She took them to the register, rung them up, and gave them their change.

"What had you so occupied? As if I don't know." Nakiyah asked with a slight smile.

"I was just reading about our ancestors during World War II." Rayna explained.

"Hm. Didn't know you made it that far."

"I can't put this thing down. It's like reading fantasy."

"Sometimes the lines between fantasy and reality are blurred – unfortunately, your ancestors had to learn that." Nakiyah said with some cracking in her voice.

Rose entered the store with her bookbag and wearing their shirt, name tag on. She put her bag behind the counter and took her place at the register. Rayna saw her smiling.

"What's got you so happy?" she asked.

"Nothing..." Rose trailed off.

"Come on. That's how I looked when your father and I started dating."

"I'm not dating anyone...yet." she insisted.

"Ooh a clue. There's a guy you like."

"I'm not saying anything else unless something happens. It's all a dream right now." Rose sighed.

"Okay...I'm here if you need to talk. I'm going to the back with Nakiyah to examine the books." Rayna said.

"You trust me alone at the front??" Rose asked with incredulousness.

"You've been here two weeks. I think you can handle it." Rayna said, grinning.

Rose sorted the incense in the cabinet. She heard a different door close and saw it was the bathroom door. She shrugged and kept looking at the incense – chakra incense, angel incense, herb incense – and took a sip of the coffee she brought with her.

She heard retching and something emptying into the toilet. Her eyes widened and she walked back, knocking on the door.

"Who's in there? Are you okay?" she asked.

"Yeah, I'm fine." Rayna said, "Must've been something I ate. I had scampi for lunch. The garlic must not've agreed with me because just the smell bothered me."

"I'll get a ginger ale from the convenience store two doors down if Nakiyah watches the register." Rayna offered.

"No, I'm fine," Rayna insisted, "I keep Pepto Bismol in my purse at all times."

Rose walked back to the register with hesitance, afraid to leave Rayna alone. But two minutes later, Rayna came out – wiping her face with a wet paper towel. She looked pale.

"Nakiyah!" Rose called.

"No, don't call her." Rayna insisted.

Nakiyah came to the front.

"What's wrong?" Nakiyah asked.

"Nothing. I just threw up my lunch." Rayna played down.

"Here," Nakiyah said, digging into her purse behind the register and pulling out a bottle of Pepto. She handed her two pink tablets.

"I'll make you a cup of ginger and peppermint tea to take them." she said, taking two bottles into the back with her.

"I didn't want her to make a fuss." Rayna bemoaned.

"She's your aunt – she wants to take care of you..and so do I."

Rayna smiled.

"You're a good kid." she said, hugging her.

"With all we've been through....you mean a lot." Rose said, looking down.

Rayna tipped her head up.

"Aw, thanks kiddo. You mean a lot to me too" Rayna said, putting her arm around her shoulders and squeezing.

Nakiyah came out with the tea and handed it to Rayna. She put the two tablets in her mouth and swallowed them wth the tea. She continued to sip it as she opened the diary and began to read.

"Good idea," Nakiyah said, "Reading will relax you. And it will prepare you for what's to come."

"Can I read too?" Rose asked.

"Of course." Rayna said, moving the leather-bound book closer to her.

As they read, they became entranced with the story.

* * *

Salem – 1722

Ivy cradled the baby in her arms as she suckled her breast. Robert was at work in the garden for the wife of their owner. Lia entered the house, holding a basket of apples, pears, berries, and corn.

"From our garden." she explained, smiling.

"You have to be quick! We don't want the missus to know!" Ivy warned.

Robert tilled the soil, inserting seeds in tiny holes, covering them, and watering them. He picked tomatoes from the plants already growing and put them in a basket. He wiped at the sweat on his face and brow. He felt like his body was on fire with the stifling heat. He couldn't imagine how his wife was managing with the baby. Suddenly, a man appeared in tan pants, a white button down shirt, and a black vest. His hair was black.

"You look thirsty." he said, holding a bucket of water.

"Yes, sir, I sure am." he replied.

"You can have water – and wouldn't it be nice to have more freedom? I can make it happen."

He extended his hand.

Robert paused in thought. If he worked in the house, there would be other slaves waving huge paper fans. The sun would be shielded. He could drink water on his breaks. When he worked in the garden, he was at his master's mercy.

He shook the man's hand. He felt his palm burn.

"We have an accord." the man said, smiling without showing his teeth. He handed him the bucket of water.

"You've earned this. I'll talk to your master." he said, going to the front door and knocking, the butler letting him in.

Robert tipped the bucket of water and drank with heartiness. The little bit left he dumped over his head, cooling himself. He took a deep breath and started pulling up carrots and celery, placing them in the harvest basket. Then he planted seeds for pumpkins and sunflowers for the fall. As he stood back up and brushed the dirt from his knees, the man was there with another bucket.

"Enjoy." he said, smiling, "You start in three days."

He handed him the bucket and walked back through the fields of wheat. Robert drank again, chugging it down and wetting his head again. He smiled. Life was getting better.

Ivy was about to put the baby in her makeshift crib when she smelled smoke. She looked at the window adjacent to her and saw fire caught on the side of her husband's house.

"No...it can't be...he wouldn't do this to me..." she stuttered.

"Quick! Hand me the baby and the book!" Lia exclaimed.

Ivy handed her the baby and put the leather-bound book in a satchel, putting it on Lia's shoulder.

"I'll run and tell the missus." Ivy said, as Lia ran for the woods.

She darted to the door but found it locked from the outside. The windows shut and locked on their own. She cowered in the opposite corner, yelling desperately for help.

Robert heard her screams and ran to the shack. Flames were bursting through the door – no way in. Tears streamed down his cheeks. He felt his palms burning. He looked at them, fear sending the hairs on his arms straight up.

What did he do?

Chapter Fifteen

Samuel stood in the middle of the circle clenching his fists. His jagged teeth ground against each other, creating a sound like scraping steel. Those heathens kept evading him and getting away from him.

'Them and their stupid powers.' he cursed.

As he stared at the circle – the candles and rocks – he got angrier. It was no longer a circle of power. It was being diminished. By a couple of witches.

"GODDAMMIT!!" He boomed.

He began breathing heavy and growling under his breath.

"Need...to..go...to...my...calm...place.." he strained out.

He closed his eyes. He felt heat around him, heard screams and the bubbles of the burning rivers.

"Ah. Home." he said, smiling.

Samuel sat in a hard chair formed slab of embers, the heat flowing through his evil form. Flames roared around him.

'Hell is a wonderful place.' he thought, grinning.

A scream echoed from across the stream of lava.

"Shut up! I can't hear myself think!" he yelled, casting a rock at the tortured being.

It hit his head and it hung limp, bone showing through the ragged skin.

"You haven't fulfilled your purpose." a voice hissed.

He turned and saw the hooded figure with red eyes, tips of horns peeking out.

"I'm working on it." Samuel grumbled.

"You've been working on it for centuries, and every time they've thwarted you." the demon growled.

"The battle will happen soon. Rayna and Nakiyah are the last of the bloodline. Nakiyah will be easy to take out. Rayna will be a challenge, but it will make her death that much sweeter." Samuel crooned, smiling his devilish grin.

"There are two more you need to kill." the demon reminded him.

"I can kill Matthew easily. Kyle is working on the daughter."

"He failed twice already." the demon said.

"He will succeed this time. He may not be the sharpest one of us, but he's learning."

"Make sure he gets the job done this time. You as well. If you don't complete the job..." the demon trailed off looking across the way.

There was a large cauldron of boiling lava with bones of victims sticking out of it. Samuel watched as another demon with yellow eyes and red skin stirred the cauldron.

"DINNER!" a voice boomed from miles away.

The demon ladled out the lava & bones into a large bowl – too large for any normal-sized being – and several others got underneath it and carried it carefully down a rocky ember path.

Samuel shuddered. It would take mere seconds for him to face his fate – and become part of the One's supper.

"Remember that, half-mortal. Your immortality is over the minute you enter that cauldron." the demon said, grinning and showing his fangs.

As he strode off, Samuel got up and rose to the surface of the earth. Time to rally the troops

* * *

Deep in the woods, in a secluded glen, stood Matthew, Rayna, and Rose.

"Try again." Rayna coaxed Rose.

Rose focused her eyes on the tree and aimed her hands at it. The tree trembled, slightly lifting up, but fell back down again.

"Anger is what will help you," Matthew said, putting his hand on her shoulder, "Think of everything that's happened since you found your power."

She closed her eyes and saw Kyle dragging her towards the bonfire – him setting fire to the diner – she saw Rayna and Nakiyah in the shaking house – she opened her eyes and they glowed amber. She aimed her hands at the tree. Rage flowed through her like an ocean tide. Her power lifted the roots from the ground, bringing the tree into the air, and she flung it into the forest across a river.

"Yes!" Rayna cheered, hugging her.

Rose's eyes still glowed amber. Rayna felt the heat of her anger. She placed her hand on Rose's heart, and her anger cooled until it disappeared.

"I don't know if I can fight..." Rose trailed off.

"When push comes to shove, you'll know what to do and when to do it. You won't be able to control yourself. But remember the difference between control and chaos – you need to combine the two to be successful." Rayna said.

"Your turn." Matthew said, patting Rayna's back.

She went and stood by the river. She visualized her ancestors – burning alive – how they started out with love, and it turned into tragedy. Her eyes were blue with red sparks when she opened them. She aimed her hands at the river and slowly brought them up. The river formed a cresting wave. She sent it through the forest, drenching everything in it's path.

"Excellent!" Matthew said, kissing her.

"Well...do your thing..." Rayna said, smiling.

"Good thing we made a firepit." he said, smirking.

"And brought hot dogs and marshmallows!" Rose added.

Matthew closed his eyes. He saw his wife, choking on her breath. The handshake. Carol burning and nothing left on the bed. No grave to visit or place flowers. Just nothing.

He opened his eyes and they glowed red with blue sparks. He aimed his hands at the firepit, with a tent of wood, and sent a stream of fire into it. It burned brightly, sparks flying.

The anger still flowed through him – like thousand degree heat in his skin.

Her ancestors caused this mess. You could fix it...if you just listen to me, a voice echoed in his head.

Matthew formed a huge fireball in his hands and held it above his head.

"Rayna, your family caused this. If it wasn't for Tituba, my wife might've lived longer." he growled, the fireball growing bigger.

"Matthew...none of us could've stopped this. They made their choices.." Rayna trailed off, shaking, "Don't make me use my power on you in front of your daughter."

"Dad...please...mom is gone. There's nothing you can do about it." Rose cried out, tears streaming down her cheeks.

"I can end the bloodline. Carol can be at peace." Matthew hissed, eyes going completely red.

Do it, a voice said, *it will all end with her death.*

As Matthew aimed the fireball, Rayna shot red and blue energy at the fireball, extinguishing it. She quickly ran over to Matthew, putting both her hands on his heart and closing her eyes. She imagined sending water that morphed into ice into his heart, cooling it with quickness.

Matthew's eyes faded to their usual blue.

"What happened?" he asked, his mind fogged.

Rayna's eyes were wet with tears.

"You were going to kill me. Nakiyah was right after all this time."

Matthew ran to Rayna and grabbed her hand.

"It won't happen again." he promised.

"How do I know that? Samuel just got into your head." she argued.

"I'll fight it! I will never let him get to me again!" he countered.

She pulled her hand away.

"You said that to me once before in another way." Rayna choked out, turning away.

"What can I do?" Matthew asked, falling to his knees, a tear sliding down his cheek.

"Leave me alone and forget me. You are what you are. I've realized I can't change that."

Rayna closed her eyes and envisioned Nakiyah's living room. When she opened her eyes, she was there.

Nakiyah stood up from her couch and hugged her.

"I tried to warn you." she said, rubbing Rayna's back.

"I know." Rayna said, sobbing into her shoulder.

Nakiyah led her over to the couch and held her as she let it all out. Her eyes glowed milky white.

If it wasn't for Rose, she could kill the bastard.

* * *

Matthew stirred the chicken noodle soup for him and Rose – tears welling in his eyes. He wandered into the kitchen and looked at the armchair where Rayna usually sat, reading the journal. He looked at the mums she bought and placed in the bay window. He collapsed on the couch, holding his head in his hands.

Samuel got in his head.

He cried out, wrapping his hands in his hair. She was his soul mate – the only woman he loved after Carol. She made life easier after they met by making him smile and becoming an influence on Rose.

He hadn't smiled in years.

Rose walked in the door and put her backpack on the stairs. She looked at her father, feeling her heart ache.

"I'll finish dinner." Rose offered.

"Nonsense," Matthew said, wiping his eyes, "I can do it."

He went back into the kitchen and ladled out the soup, cutting fresh dill over the bowls. He put them on the table, and they sat down.

Rose blew on her spoonfuls of soup with hesitance, missing Rayna as she looked at her empty chair.

"I miss her, too." Matthew commented, sipping his chicken noodle soup.

"Do something, Dad." Rose pleaded.

"I don't know what to do." he admitted.

Rose paused in thought.

"Well, there's one thing you can do." she suggested, whispering something in his ear.

Matthew half-smiled.

"Maybe that would work." he admitted.

Later that day, they traveled to the site of Samuel's house. Matthew laid two dozen pink roses at the place where he thought Tituba's shack might've been as Rose filmed with her smartphone.

"History makes us who we are," he mused aloud, "It shapes our future, and we can't control what it will be. The best we can do is make peace with it. I had a hard time of dealing with my wife's death. It wasn't until I met Rayna that I was able to smile again. She made me laugh, and she mothered my daughter, despite Rose's resistance..."

Rose shook her head and rolled her eyes.

"I miss her every day, and it's only right that I honor the history behind this town that Rayna loves so much. It's become a home to me too – one I never want to leave. It's all thanks to this amazing woman who taught me to love again, and I can only hope she sees this and forgives me for my blind bitterness. Rayna, I love you with the depths of my heart, and life is empty without you. Please come home."

Rose clicked and posted it to YouTube and Matthew's social media.

"Will it work?" he asked.

"Dad, if it doesn't...you weren't meant to be."

An hour later, it went viral – getting 50,000 views, including Rayna. She showed Nakiyah, who shook her head.

"It's your choice. It's up to what you believe." Nakiyah said, walking away.

Rayna wiped the tears from her eyes.

What was she going to do?

* * *

Rayna unlocked the door to *Midnight Tomes* and walked in, holding a bag of perfume and makeup from a beauty store. Retail therapy always helped.

When she looked at the counter, her jaw dropped.

There were ten cups of coffee from her favorite coffee and a bouquet of a dozen yellow roses on the counter. Rayna approached them with caution, waiting for a fireball to appear. She looked behind the counter and saw no one. She lifted the lid of one cup and sniffed.

Pumpkin Spice latte.

Ten of them.

Rayna half-smiled and shook her head. Matthew was trying very hard. She heard the door jingle and turned around to see him standing there.

"I wanted to make sure you were caffeinated enough for today." Matthew excused, hands in his pockets.

"And the roses?" Rayna asked.

"Well, I wanted to give you something that attempted to match your beauty." he replied.

"Sweet talk won't work on me." she argued, trying not to smile.

"You saw the video." he accused.

"How do you know?" she asked.

"Otherwise you wouldn't be biting your cheeks to hide a smile." he answered, walking over to her.

Rayna backed against the counter, almost spilling the coffee.

"Careful – those lattes took a lot of work." Matthew said, grinning.

"I wouldn't want to upset the barista." Rayna murmured, sipping a cup.

Matthew stroked her cheek.

"The house is empty without you," he admitted, "We sit there every night, looking at your empty chair as we eat. The arm chair misses you. I don't have any Indigo Girls or Sarah McLachlan to listen to."

"Can you live without it?" she whispered.

"No, I can't." he said, pulling her to him.

"How can I trust you?" Rayna asked, reluctant to touch him.

"If I ever do it again, I don't deserve to live. I give you permission to kill me." he offered.

"What?!" she exclaimed.

"Look, I know what I am. Samuel will always be trying to turn me. If he does, you can kill me." Matthew said with blunt honesty.

"How am I going to do that?" Rayna choked out.

"You want to live. You want your ancestors to be at peace, like I want Carol to be at peace. The only way to do that is to destroy Samuel and all his henchmen. If I become one of them..." he paused, "...turn me to ash."

Tears streamed down Rayna's face.

"You're my..." she began.

"Say it." he whispered.

"My beloved." she finished.

"And you're mine." Matthew confessed.

He kissed her gently at first, then becoming more passionate. Rayna hesitated to encourage him any further, but feeling the electricity go through her, she wrapped her arms around his neck. She wrapped her hands in his hair and pulled his hips against hers, feeling his hardness.

"Later." she whispered against his lips.

"I'll hold you to that." he promised, "Enjoy your coffee, and put the roses in water before they die."

"They won't die, and neither will you." Rayna swore.

"Time will tell – we can't predict our future." he reminded her.

"I can't kill you." she said, reaching for his hand.

Matthew squeezed hers.

"If you have to, you will." he said, leaving.

Rayna cut the stems of the roses and threw them away, putting them in a blue porcelain vase, tears still flowing down her cheeks. Nakiyah walked in and came over to her, rubbing her back.

"If it has to be, it will be." she confessed to her.

"Can't you see?" Rayna asked.

"No. I'm sorry." she replied, taking her hand.

As a customer walked in, Rayna wiped at her face with a tissue and moved the coffee behind the counter. Nakiyah listened to the customer's questions and led her to the stacks. Rayna stood behind the counter, waiting for the transaction.

It was unlike the transaction that might take place on Halloween. That scared her.

* * *

Rose stirred a pot of stew and took a pan of roasted root vegetables out of the oven, seasoned with herbs de Provence, salt, and pepper. Matthew walked in half-hearted, trying to smile and failing.

"Smells good." he commented.

"It's ready, so I hope you have a good appetite." Rose said.

"Not really, but I'll try."

Rose stopped stirring.

"Yeah...I haven't been able to eat enough since -"

" - the incident in the glen." Matthew finished.

"I don't get it. You swore to her you'd never hurt her." Rose murmured, crying.

"Samuel has a great amount of power. He infiltrated my mind by making me believe every thought about the whole curse." Matthew explained.

"Is it a curse?" Rose asked.

"I don't know what else to call it." Matthew sighed, sitting down at the table.

Rose put their bowls of stew on their placemats and put the platter of root vegetables in the middle of the table. As they picked at their food, silence permeated the room.

No laughter, no smiles brightened the house. Rayna's voice didn't echo through the hallways. Her witch silhouette mug sat in the dish drainer, empty. A bouquet of sunflowers was all that remained of her beauty in the center of the kitchen table.

"Dad, can you sing me our sadness song?" Rose asked.

Matthew half-smiled.

"Of course sweetie..."

"Always look on the bright side of life...

Always look on the light side of life...

If life seems jolly rotten, there's something you've forgotten..

And that's to laugh and smile and dance and sing..

If you're feeling in the dumps, don't be silly chumps...

Just purse your lips and whistle, that's the thing...

And always look on the bright side of life..."

Rose stared into her bowl of half-eaten stew.

"I'm sorry, dad. It didn't help."

"That usually perks you right up, unless you want me to rap some of Hamilton." a voice said.

Rose and Matthew snapped their heads up and looked in the doorway.

Rayna.

Matthew smiled, and Rose ran to hug her.

"Want some stew?" Matthew asked.

"Sounds good to me. I'm starving. I skipped lunch because a group of tourists came in, and we had to help them explore our shelves. I also had to explain the herb cabinet." Rayna explained casually.

Rose scooped her out some stew, and Rayna took her seat at the table, eating voraciously.

"Are you back for good?" Rose asked.

Rayna looked up at Matthew.

"If it's okay with your father..." she trailed off.

"More than anything." he murmured.

Blocks away, Nakiyah opened her eyes and frowned.

Rayna didn't realize what was ahead.

Chapter Sixteen

Rose walked through the crunchy orange and red leaves to their glen in the woods. She felt the stability of earth within her. She carried with her a candles the colors of the seven chakras – red, orange, yellow, green, light blue, indigo, and purple - and a Tibetan singing bowl. As she reached the clearing, she listened to the river babbling in the distance. In the ripples, she heard Rayna's voice: "Be careful." She paused in shock – she was never able to hear the water like Rayna.

She kneeled by the river, staring.

She heard nothing else.

Maybe she imagined it.

She put the candles in a circle, lit them, and sat cross-legged on the ground, holding the bowl in her palm, tapping it with a wooden stick and then running it rapidly around the rim, a golden sound emanating. She closed her eyes and continued, feeling energy vibrating through her like a starburst.

Just then, her mind darkened. A vision came to her – burned forests, people looting, murder victims in the streets, whole hoards of women being herded behind gates and set afire with flame throwers.

She opened her eyes, hyperventilating and crying.

"So you see what we want." she heard a voice say.

Rose looked and saw Kyle, his eyes glowing red. He stalked towards her, his palms sparking.

"Armageddon will come. Any of your kind will be wiped out. Fire will reign. Earth will be a starved, barren place. And you...you will die."

He shot a flame at her. She froze for a second before she felt something rise up in her. She wove her hands and petrified vines rose from the earth, entangling him.

"You bitch!" he cursed, "What the fuck are you?!"

"I'm your worst nightmare." she growled.

Out of nowhere, a gust of wind turned into a cyclone. The vines receded, and the cyclone picked him up.

"I'll get you!! If I can get the fuck off this storm!" he cursed as it took him away.

* * *

The storm dumped Kyle in the middle of the woods – acres away – and he landed hard on the ground.

"My fucking tailbone!" he exclaimed, struggling to his feet.

Samuel appeared in a burst of flame.

"You let her get away again!" he cursed at Kyle.

"You don't understand -" Kyle began.

"Of course I do! You're a dumbass!"

"No...that bitchy aunt...she interfered." Kyle stuttered.

"WHAT?!" Samuel boomed.

"I got carried me away on a cyclone!" he explained.

"Goddammit," Samuel cursed, "This isn't good."

"What does it mean?" Kyle asked.

Samuel paced the woods, his brow furrowed in concentration, muttering to himself.

"How is it Rose?! How is it that straight A, choir singing, artsy bitch?!" Kyle exclaimed.

"She's as powerful as the rest of them," he continued, pacing, "She will bolster their ability to defeat us."

"Go back to your parents," Samuel advised, "Keep going to school. She won't say a word because no one would believe it. I'll find you when I need to."

Samuel disappeared in another burst of flame.

Kyle looked at his burned clothes. His parents would wonder what the hell happened.

He'd go to Luke's place. He owned appropriate clothes. He'd just say he fell in the woods and needed clean clothes.

His eyes burned.

He'd kill her. She was a challenge now.

* * *

Rose rushed into the house, candles and bowl in her messenger bag, panting. Rayna and Matthew were on the couch, talking. They looked up, saw her wide eyes, and ran over to her. Rayna held her close, and Rose's breathing slowed.

"What happened, honey?" Matthew asked running her back.

"I – I don't know..." Rose stuttered.

"Start from the beginning. That's the only way to begin." Rayna said.

"I – I saw the future." Rose admitted.

"The remnant earth?" Nakiyah asked.

"Yeah. And Kyle told me their plan."

They all sat on the couch and listened to her – the terrifying plan the hoard had for the world, starting in Salem.

"Dear God." Rayna breathed, shaking.

"We can fight this." Nakiyah said with simplicity.

"How? They want to bring on Armageddon! He's helped by hell!"

"He's a figure of Hell. What's down below never gets involved. They chose him to start this apocalypse. They saw the potential in him."

Rayna clutched Rose and Matthew's hands.

"This isn't just for our lives..." she trailed off.

"It's for the world." Rose finished, taking a deep breath.

"So we have to be ready, at our strongest and with no fear." Nakiyah warned them.

"We will be." Matthew growled.

The fire roared. And upstairs, the shower turned on.

In their garden, a single yellow rose pushed its way up from the earth and opened its petals.

Outside a breeze blew, ruffling the leaves on the trees.

They all looked at each other. They were ready.

* * *

Salem – 1944

Patricia took the chicken leg quarters out of the oven. They were sprin-kled with salt, pepper, and rosemary. She scooped mashed potatoes onto each dish, along with some fresh beets from the Victory garden, and one leg quarter. She set each plate on the table, along with a cold bottle of Coke, and some napkins. The doorbell rang. She opened the door, and there stood William, dressed in a white button down shirt, Dockers, and dress shoes. His dirty blonde hair was slicked back and his eyes contained a fire.

"Dinner's on the table." she said, smiling.

She led him to the table in the kitchen and lit a candle, turning the lights off.

"Ooh, atmosphere." he said, smirking.

"I thought it would be a nice touch for a first date."

As they ate, they talked about the different radio shows they liked, what William did before he was in the Marines..

"I live with my aunt and uncle here. They work in a grocery store in town." he explained.

"What about your parents?" Patricia asked.

"They died when I was a youngster, and my grandma, who raised me, died after I graduated college. So I enrolled in the army. Since then, I just float from one family member to another. Never had a chance to set down roots."

"Well, now, maybe you can." she murmured.

He saw the rosiness of her blush in the candlelight.

"Man, I'm full. How's about we relax on the couch in the living room and put the radio on?" he suggested.

"Okay." Patricia agreed.

He offered his arm and she took it, both of them taking a seat on the couch after Patricia put on a music radio show. Frank Sinatra began to sing "Oh, What It Seemed to Be" at the Copa Cabana – it was a live show.

William turned her head towards his and looked deep in her eyes. His glowed red. Hers were silver.

"What are you?" she gasped.

"I want you. For life." he said, stroking her hair, "You've got charm like Gene Tierney, curves that would make any man drool, and - " he dipped her head back and kissed her neck, "You have bewitched me."

"William." she breathed.

Lightning struck outside and it began to pour.

"Thunderstorms," he whispered, "Sexy."

"My grandmother would kill me." she protested.

"Let her kill us both. We'll die happy." he said, chuckling.

As the storm got stronger, they became one.

They spent a wonderful month together, going to restaurants, window shopping, going to the Halloween Festival.

Then William got called up to Poland. Patricia cried as she watched him leave on a ship from Boston Harbor.

Four weeks later, Patricia sat on her doctor's table.

"Well...you're pregnant. I don't want to know how, but you know you need to be married now." her doctor said, pacing the floor.

"My fiance is in service right now." she told him.

"Get him back as soon as possible. You can't risk this becoming a scandal." he advised her.

When Patricia got home, she took out a sheet of stationary and her pen.

How would she tell him?

Chapter Seventeen

Stamford, CT – 1997

Tiffany walked down the dark street to her house. She held a college application in her hand – Harvard. She rolled her eyes. As she opened the door and walked in, her mother, Sonya, looked up.

"Did you finish the application?" she asked.

"Yes." Tiffany huffed.

"What about the essay?" Sonya asked.

"Still working on it."

"Don't forget the early deadline is soon. You HAVE to get that in!"

"I KNOW – it's a tradition." Tiffany begrudged.

"Well, don't you want to be pre-med?" her mother asked, "You could make so much money!"

Her father, Winston, walked in with briefcase in hand.

"How did that asbestos case go?" Sonya asked.

"The company won, so I did my job." he sighed.

He flopped his briefcase down by the stairs and trudged towards the kitchen.

'Turkey, mashed potatoes, and corn. Things never change.'

"Jesus, this is my life..." Tiffany groaned, head in hand.

"You have a good life!" Sonya pointed out.

Tiffany tore up her college application and ran out of the house, slamming the door.

She dashed down the street, hearing her mother yelling after her.

That's why she was seeing Justin behind their backs. He gave her what they never did – love.

Someone average.

As she turned the corner to head to his place, knowing her parents would ground her for coming in late, she needed to see him.

And they couldn't stop her – she was 18 going on 19 in August.

Once Tiffany got away from them, that was it. Even if she had to take a waitress job.

"Life has many detours, doesn't it?" a voice asked.

She turned and saw an older man, in a jean jacket, white t-shirt, and matching jeans.

"Yeah, it does." she admitted.

"We strive so hard for freedom when we're young – only to have it taken away." he continued.

"You have no idea." she said, chuckling, "I wish I had a different life."

"Just close your eyes and imagine what you want."

He held out his hand.

She clasped it and closed her eyes. She saw her parents disappearing into darkness. She felt a burn in her palm.

When she opened them, the man was grinning without showing his teeth.

He turned around and headed back down the street. She stared for a minute and smiled. Now she could celebrate with Justin.

She reached his house and found him in the pool, going up and down the length of it.

"Hey sexy." she greeted, smirking.

"Come for something?" he asked, winking.

"You know it." she replied, "But I have no swimsuit."

He pulled her into the pool.

She burst into laughter, but he kissed her, stroking her damp hair.

She felt energy filling her, her endorphins spiking. She kissed him with more passion, clutching his hair. Then he went stiff as a board. Her jaw was agape. He floated on the surface of the water. Her heart raced like a mudder at a rainy Kentucky Derby.

"Got what you needed?" a voice asked.

She turned and saw that same man.

"What the hell happened?" she asked.

"I gave you a gift." he replied, smiling with jagged teeth.

Tiffany ran from the house, tears streaking her face. When she reached her place, the house was in flames.

Her parents weren't on the street. They were nowhere to be found.

She felt chills of terror go through her.

The second deaths of the night.

She took her keys from her purse and jumped in her '89 Corvette.

Salem wasn't far away.

She could hide in a town like that.

* * *

Tiffany stood outside the high school with Kyle's arm around her, him smoking a cigarette and sneaking a flask every so often. She was wearing a short khaki shirt, a tied white button-down shirt – exposing her midriff – and gold hoop earrings. She wore a ruby ring on her finger.

"Aren't we a little young for this?" she asked, looking at the ring.

She felt him take a hold of her wrist and clench it hard. She bit her lip to keep from crying out.

"You don't want me to get upset do you?" Kyle whispered, kissing her neck.

"No..." she whimpered.

"Then why won't you fuck me?" he growled.

"I just...want to wait for the right time." she said, pulling him to her and kissing him.

She felt his energy go into her and she almost puked in his mouth. It felt like being filled with poison – a little at a time to make your death linger.

"NOW." he growled.

"There's no place -"

He didn't let her finish, dragging her through the gym and into the locker room. She wriggled away from him and dashed for the door. He caught her by the wrist but she flew around to face him and punched him so hard he fell back against the lockers, his lip bleeding, a tooth on the floor.

"Weights, asshole." she spat, running out the door.

She rushed to her car and started it up, heading back to her apartment to pack up.

There had to be another town.

* * *

Asbury Park - 2018

Tiffany managed to get a job at a local restaurant and an apartment in the boardwalk area. Then she met Marina. She had brown hair in curls, blue eyes, and olive toned skin. Her lips were full and rosy pink. They smiled at each other.

"Can I get you another drink?" Tiffany asked, smirking.

"Oh yeah...I'm thirsty." Marina replied, touching her hand.

"I know just what to quench it." Tiffany whispered, heading to the ladies room.

A few minutes later, Marina followed. They kissed with passion and fervor in the bathroom stall, hands squeezing and caressing flesh, Tiffany pulling up Marina's shirt to see she wasn't wearing a bra. She sucked on her breast, eliciting a moan. Marina turned her around and pushed her against the door.

She pulled down Tiffany's skirt and panties, her mouth lowering to her nether regions, her tongue stroking her walls and clit. Tiffany stifled a torturous moan, clutching at the metal walls. She felt a rush of power going through her. Marina reached her hand up and manipulated her breast, causing Tiffany to almost scream.

"Come for me." Marina husked.

Tiffany looked into her eyes as she came, Marina covering her mouth.

Marina's eyes were glowing silver.

Purple and silver sparks and light flew around them, creating an aura of unrelenting power.

Tiffany heaved breath, staring at Marina.

"What...are you?" she asked.

"The same as you. And I want you. Forever." Marina whispered, nibbling her ear.

Tiffany grabbed her and kissed her, her tongue probing her mouth. Marina growled into her mouth. Tiffany reached her hand down and stroked Marina's depths, Marina moaned, clutching at Tiffany's shoulders. Tiffany sped up her motions, rubbing around Marina's clit, as she reached climax, stifling a yell. Marina slumped against her.

"Where do you live?" Marina breathed.

"Down the street." Tiffany murmured.

"Take me there." Marina asked, kissing her with gentleness.

"Follow me." Tiffany whispered.

Tiffany told her manager she didn't feel well and was leaving for the night. Marina followed. As they entered her apartment, they stripped down and laid in bed, spooning each other.

"Could this work?" Marina asked.

"I don't know..." Tiffany trailed off.

Tiffany rolled over on top of her and kissed her again, trailing kisses down her body.

She didn't have a clue what was going on – but it was special.

* * *

The next day, Tiffany and Marina strolled the boardwalk. They got Cuban food for lunch – Tiffany got the ropa vieja and Marina got the pork sandwich.

"So where do you come from?" Marina asked.

"Stamford, Connecticut. I had it all – wealth, was gonna be pre-med." Tiffany replied.

"Then why did you come here to wait tables?" Marina asked.

"I was sick of being forced into a life I didn't want."

Marina paused in thought.

"What?" Tiffany asked.

"Nothing. I was just thinking."

"I was in Salem for a while. I met a guy. We were engaged," Tiffany explained, looking at the ring on her finger, "But it didn't work out. I moved here for a change of scenery, and I was alone."

"Until you met me." Marina concluded.

"Your eyes, your lips, your body. I'm drunk on you." Tiffany said, ending with a smirk.

"You're not so bad yourself." Marina replied, smiling back.

"I'm plain." Tiffany complained, sipping her ginger ale.

"No," Marina countered, "You have hair like the sun, eyes like milk chocolate, legs so curved and abs so tight you could be carved from marble."

She stroked Tiffany's thigh under the table. Tiffany closed her eyes and let out a shaky breath.

"Let's pay and go watch the ocean." Marina suggested, putting cash on the table.

They walked outside and found a bench facing the ocean. Marina put her arm around Tiffany's shoulders, and Tiffany rested her head on her.

Marina stroked Tiffany's sun toned blonde hair. Tiffany turned and kissed her cheek. Marina kissed her hard, pulling her hair slightly. Tiffany moaned and stroked her mouth, caressing her breast through the tank top. Marina pulled away breathless, her eyes glowing again. Tiffany still wondered why that happened, but she would ask her at the right moment.

"Let's go home." she husked, massaging Tiffany's soft spot, "Or else I'll have to do you right here."

She pulled Tiffany's head back, exposing her neck and kissing it slowly, sucking on a spot and leaving a mark.Tiffany let out a sensual growl, grabbing Marina's hand.

As she led her back to the apartment, two guys with beer bellies, wearing white t-shirts and jeans and red hats passed them.

"Fuckin' dykes." the brown haired man cursed, "Can't you keep that shit off our boardwalk?"

"Excuse me?" Marina asked.

"Babe, let's just go.." Tiffany asked, pulling her hand.

"Call us whatever the fuck you want – if you follow idiots who lambaste anyone that goes against the grain. We're people, too. And we deserve respect like any other human being. So go get your fill at whatever hole-in-the-wall you frequent and drown your addled minds." Marina snapped.

Tiffany's eyes went wide.

The men mumbled and wandered off, pulling their red hats down and pulling up their jeans that were exposing their cracks.

"I've...never..." Tiffany trailed off.

"This is your first time dating a woman?" Marina asked, taking her hand.

"Yeah. My first love was someone from my school," Tiff began as they headed to her apartment, telling Marina about the average, beautiful boy she loved.

"So what happened?" Marina asked.

"A huge mistake – then I went to his house. We kissed, and the next thing I knew he was floating in the pool." she replied with tears in her eyes.

"Baby, how often has this happened?" Marina asked.

"Every time I do it. I traveled from town to town, fleeing whenever it happened. It looked like their hearts stopped, so they could never trace anything. They just assumed their heart gave out in a quickie."

Tiffany paused, "I don't know why I told you that. You probably think I'm a freak."

"Tiff, why do you think sparks flew and light ignited when we made love?" Marina asked.

"I don't know." Tiffany admitted, as she unlocked her door.

Marina pulled her close and whispered in her ear, "We're both demons."

Tiffany backed into her apartment, shaking.

"I'm not going to do anything to you – don't be so scared. I've showed you I love you." Marina crooned, trying to calm her down.

"I'm not a demon..." Tiffany insisted.

"That's why you kill people. It's what you were given," Marina paused, "Did a man shake your hand?"

"How do you know that?" Tiffany asked, tripping over a dumbbell on the floor.

"Did he promise you what you wanted?"

"Kind of." Tiffany said, trembling.

"That was your deal. What happened to your parents?" she asked.

"The house burned down. They died." Tiffany said, tears streaming down her cheek.s

"Your ability to kill with sex was the price." Marina informed her.

Tiffany plopped down on the couch and clutched the back of it to hold herself up.

"How...did you become this?" Tiffany asked.

Marina let out a deep breath and asked, "Do you have any wine?"

"I have a bottle of white in the fridge." Tiffany replied.

Marina poured them both a full glass and brought them over to the coffee table, handing Tiffany her glass.

"I was with a strong-willed woman. Very tough. She often grabbed me hard and bruised me whenever I talked to any woman. When I didn't have dinner on the table, she backhanded me. I had so many black eyes, and each time I had to say I banged into something."

Marina shed her own tears.

"One night, walking home from 8 hours of bartending, I met a man., and he shook my hand. Next thing I knew, there was a message on the answering machine. She had been pushed into the incinerator by an angry, homophobic man at work." Marina choked out, sipping her wine with shaky hands, "I felt guilty ever since."

Tiffany and Marina both put down their glasses out of instinct as they hugged each other. Tiffany pulled away and looked into Marina's eyes. They burned bright silver, sparks alighting in her irises. Marina kissed Tiffany with passion, pulling her pants down with her panties. Her mouth trailed licks and kisses down her abdomen as she pulled her shirt off.

"Is this right?" Tiffany asked, "At this moment?"

"I want to erase any trauma from your memory. I want to make you scream it all away." Marina husked, delving into her soft regions with her tongue.

Ten minutes later, Tiffany screamed, her fingers entwined in Marina's hair.

For those few minutes, she forgot everything.

* * *

Salem – 1947

William walked in from a hard day of work at the hardware store. He stripped off his rain jacket and hung it on the hook to dry. He heard a wailing baby and his three year-old daughter in the kitchen. William walked in and smelled lentil soup.

"We're having that again?" he complained.

"Don't complain. This is what I had to work with." Patricia said, wiping the sweat from her brow.

William pulled at the collar of his starched uniform and looked at the air conditioning unit.

It was off.

"It's hot as hell in here!" he yelled.

"We have to conserve energy!" Patricia argued.

She turned to the soup and stirred it before taking out the milk and pouring William a small glass.

"I get a juice glass full of milk?" he asked.

"The children need it – it builds up their bones and teeth."

He gulped it down and sat at the kitchen table.

"Daddy, story!" the three year-old demanded.

"Not now. Daddy is tired." he said, yawning.

"Story!!" she screeched.

The baby heard her and started crying again. Patricia picked it up and soothed it, whispering to it.

"Just tell her a story, William. It won't kill you."

His eyes glowed red. He got up and stared her down.

"Electricity, milk, food – what next, life in boxes on the street?!" he boomed.

"Baby, I'm just trying to make a life for us that we can afford..."

"I can't take living on nothing anymore. This job at the hardware store is murder." he growled, stalking towards her.

"William...what happened to you?" Patricia asked, backing up.

"I know what you are – rumors are going around town. You work in a tarot reading store in town. You go under the name Madame Rayna, but everyone knows who you are." he hissed, beginning to raise his arms.

"What are you?" she stammered.

"I got a promise of fortune and freedom – and I intend to get it." he said raising his hands, fire in his palms.

"Don't do this..." Patricia pleaded.

"It's too late. I made my deal." Robert growled.

"Nakiyah, take your sister and go down two houses. Knock on the door and run in!" Patricia yelled, putting the baby in a small stroller.

Nakiyah ran with her little legs out the door, pushing the stroller. William turned to throw the fire at them, but as they left the house, Pa-

tricia whipped up winds that spread the fire to the ceilings. She waved her hand and the door slammed and locked. She aimed her hands at the windows, and the wave of power she sent made them thick and hard. William glared at her.

"We die together." Patricia said, whipping up the winds stronger.

The fire surrounded them and engulfed the house, murmurs and screams permeating the street. A neighbor held the baby and the three-year old stared at the house, whimpering. Her eyes glowed blue and suddenly the fire died down.

Madame Rayna was dead, but Madame Rose lived on.

* * *

The next night, Tiffany was walking home from work. She was two blocks away from her apartment. She hummed "Cake by the Ocean" by DNCE, the last song that played at the restaurant before she left. She felt a hand on her shoulder, gripping her tight. The person turned her around and pushed her against a wall.

It was the two guys from the other day.

"She's a pretty one." the brown haired man slurred, "Too bad she's a lesbo."

"I bet I can turn you." the raven haired guy said, pushing Tiffany against the wall.

Marina appeared in front of them, her eyes glowing silver. The brown haired man grabbed Marina, holding her back. She forced the guy back with power, and he fell on the boardwalk. He stared up at her, shaking. She raised her hands and thunder rumbled. Lightning went into both of their bodies, electrocuting them. They convulsed, their tongues hanging out of their mouths, until they fell to the ground, black burn marks all over their bodies. Marina looked up and saw Tiffany trembling, curled against the building. Her eyes went back to their blue shade, and she rushed over to Tiffany, hugging her.

"I'm so sorry, baby." she said, stroking her hair.

"What was that?" Tiffany whispered.

"I...control storms." Marina admitted.

Tiffany's tears streamed down her cheeks.

"Can you do that to me?" she asked, shivering.

"No," Marina paused, "But my power went through you, and yours combined with it when we made love."

"So...what does that mean?"

Marina looked deep in her brown eyes and took her hands.

"You're mine. And I'm yours. Forever." she replied, kissing her forehead.

"I just want to go home." Tiffany whimpered, clutching Marina.

"We will, baby. Come on. I'll take you to my place." Marina replied.

She led her down three blocks to a brownstone apartment building. As they walked up the stairs, Marina clutched Tiffany, her body weak with trauma.

As they entered the apartment, Tiffany looked around. Marina had nature photos on canvas on the walls. The bed was in the center of the room, the bedspread turquoise and silver. The kitchen had marble counters, a coffee station, and various appliances on the counter – a Vitamix, a crockpot, a mixer.

"I'll get you a pair of pajamas." Marina said, taking Tiffany over to the bed and sitting her down on it.

She got out a pajamas and undressed her, slipping the pants and shirt on her. Then she got into her own pair. Marina helped Tiffany into the bed, draping the comforter over her and laid next to her. Tiffany wept into her shoulder as Marina stroked her back and hair. She held her close, whispering words of love in her ears until they both fell asleep.

Marina was used to the hatred. Tiffany wasn't.

And they couldn't go to the police.

After all, the assholes were dead.

* * *

When Tiffany awoke the next morning, she smelled coffee and waffles. She sat up and walked over to the marble counter, taking a seat on a stool.

"Light syrup or regular? Or do I really need to ask?" Marina joked.

"Light." Tiffany whispered, wrapping her arms around herself.

Marina turned and saw her diminished form. She took the last waffle out of the iron, set it on one of their plates, and led Tiffany over to the couch.

"I'm sorry for what you went through, and, as you saw, I'd do anything to protect you. But I can't protect you from the hatred. We all experience it. I know it must've been a shock the first time, but it's all around. The country is being turned into a dangerous place. The most we can do is be better people and do what we can to make it more accepting & loving."

Tiffany cried into Marina's shoulder as Marina clutched her to her body, stroking her back.

"Why don't you tell me how you got here? Maybe it'll ease your guilt to get it all out." Marina suggested.

"I was a popular girl at school – debate team, choir, student council, band, drama club. I had it all. Until I met...him. The night I saw our house burning, I packed my bags and took off in my Honda. I sold it at a car dealer and walked to the Hyundai place a few stops down the highway. I bought a flame red Hyundai. I took off, terrified they'd tie me to it.

Then I met this guy. He was charming at first. But before long, he started beating me and assaulting me, leaving me broken. I was so scared of him, I'd do anything to keep him calm. Until he tried to get me to join the other demons...led by that guy. I went to this bookstore I knew was owned by one of the targets of their hatred. She was so friendly and helpful. She gave me this bracelet, and it gave me the courage to fight back. He...tried to assault me. But by then, I was spending hours in the gym, trying to regain my strength. I fought him off, packed my stuff, I took my Hyundai here and never looked back."

"What was the guy's name?" Marina asked, kissing her forehead.

"Kyle."

Marina paused in shock.

"Do you mean – Kyle O'Hara?"

"That's Samuel's right-hand man." Marina marveled.

"Who's Samuel?" Tiffany asked.

"The man who makes deals. In return for half our souls. Then he gives us some kind of power he thinks will be to his advantage, convinced he'll recruit us." Marina explained.

"How many rebel?" Tiffany asked.

"Not many. Only those whose power match his can break his influence." Marina said.

Her eyes narrowed and glowed silver.

"If either one of them ever touches you -" she began.

"Calm down," Tiffany said, stroking Marina's arms, "They haven't found me, and I doubt they will. I'm not under their control anymore."

Marina stared at the floor, her brow furrowed.

"We have to go back and fight." she admitted.

"What do you mean?!" Tiffany asked, chills going through her.

Marina grabbed her shoulders with gentleness.

"I know you're scared, but you're stronger than you think. Think about it – you escaped their grasp. Your power matches theirs, just like mine does. I believe we can harness your power for good use. I have a plan if you'll listen to me."

"I don't know if I can..." Tiffany trailed off.

"You CAN," Marina insisted, "What you need is anger. It'll give you more power and more reason to fight."

Marina brushed her hands over Tiffany's face and closed her eyes.

"Picture yesterday. Picture Kyle."

Tiffany began to tremble and cry.

"That's a natural reaction. But imagine if that happened to me."

Tiffany's trembling became stronger. Her fists clenched. Her jaw ground her teeth together. When she opened her eyes, they were purple with silver sparks.

"That's what you need." Marina said, kissing her.

As they made out, Tiffany felt the heat go from her eyes. She clutched Marina's waist and pulled away, gasping for air.

"Come on. Have breakfast and some coffee, and I'll tell you my plan." Marina said, going back over to the counter and sitting down.

Tiffany sat down beside her and listened to Marina, her smile widening with each word.

Those half-demon scum suckers were in for it.

Chapter Eighteen

Matthew had a pearly smile on his face and a thermos of coffee in one of his hands. He was wearing khaki pants with his jacket half-way open, a white button down shirt underneath. He saw an older woman looking at the dairy section.

"Do you need help?" he asked.

"What's the difference between cage-free and organic eggs?" she asked him.

"Cage-free means they're allowed to wander around the farm, and organic means they're fed differently from other chickens – more natural food." He explained..

"Thank you, young man," she said, smiling.

As he left, he saw her pick up the cage free eggs. He smiled wider.

Matthew passed a few of his co-workers, greeted them, and fist bumped them. As he entered his office, he hung up his jacket and sat down, sipping his coffee. He opened the internet browser and his email account. As he googled the popularity of kombucha and its trends over the past year, he saw an email pop up about a staff meeting. Matthew frowned. He was supposed to pick up Rose from theater practice – they were putting on "Romeo and Juliet", and she was Juliet.

They announced the play a week ago, and she immediately tried out for the part. She waited three days for a response, and, when she got it, she smiled like Matthew. She practiced her lines for hours at night in her room. He couldn't let her down or ask Rayna to leave the bookstore. He responded to the email in decline and deleted it.

He went about his day, taking notes on a legal pad and printing graphs and charts on organic, fair trade trends. When five o'clock came, he put his jacket on, grabbed his thermos, and shut down his laptop – closing it and putting it in a case.

As he drove to the high school, he felt a sense of foreboding over the next day. He shook it off, convinced it was just his paranoia over everything that was going on.

* * *

The next day, Matthew was sitting at his desk, taking a breather. He sipped a cup of tea he got from the cafe next door and perused the newspaper.

Amy, the produce manager, popped her head in.

"Lester sent me to tell you to come to his office." she said, averting her eyes.

"I'll be there." Matthew said, getting up.

He strode down the hall and into Lester's office, sitting down and waiting for him to get off the phone. When he did, Matthew addressed him.

"Is this about the numbers I sent you yesterday?" Matthew asked.

"No, it's not." Lester said, taking a pill out of a bottle and swallowing it.

Matthew looked at the bottle and saw it was Xanax.

"We have to cut costs. Profits are down, and we can't afford some things anymore." Lester said.

"Do you need me to scale down some of the inventory?" Matthew asked, "I know we have an overstock of yogurt, and the milk has been running down its dates..."

Lester took off his glasses and rubbed his eyes.

"We have to let you go."

"What?" Matthew asked, jaw agape, "I worked here for a year – I've had exemplary reports! Why don't you cut some of the part timers? Or even make my job a shared job and just lower the salary?!"

"I've gone over this as many ways as I know how, and I'm sorry." Lester concluded, motioning to the door.

Matthew felt heat rising in his eyes, but he took a deep breath and suppressed it.

"That's bullshit," he growled, "All you care about is the bottom line. I better get my severance pay in the mail."

Lester glared at him.

"If you attended the staff meeting, you would've known about the layoffs." he muttered, shoving another pill in his mouth.

Matthew glared back at him for a second, mouth opening, but he left, slamming the door.

He grabbed his jacket from his office and stormed out the door, careening his car back home. When he flew through the front door of his house, Rayna looked up, shaken. She put down her book and walked over.

"What happened?" she asked.

Matthew explained the situation to her, and she hugged him.

"Sweetie, I'm so sorry." she said, squeezing him.

"I can't handle anyone touching me right now." he said in a deep voice, his fists clenched.

"Sit down in your recliner. I'll get you something to help you." she insisted.

He did as she said, taking off his jacket and shoes and leaning back in the recliner. In a few minutes she came in the living room and handed him a hot mug.

"This is lavender tea with honey and lemon. Inhale the steam and sip it." Rayna instructed.

He inhaled the steam and let out a deep breath, feeling his anger pull back a little. As Matthew sipped the tea, he felt his anger subside substantially. By the time he finished it, he was calm.

"Better?" Rayna asked.

"Yeah. Thanks, babe."

Rose walked in the open door, seeing the hinges slightly lifted off the wood frame.

"What's going on?" she asked, stepping into the room with hesitance.

"Your father lost his job." Rayna said with softness.

Rose walked over to her father and wrapped her arms around him. He did the same to her, stroking her hair.

"What are we gonna do?" she murmured between tears, "Can we keep the house? Can I go to college? What about the bills?"

"Don't worry – we'll be okay. Rayna is working still, and I'll figure something out." Matthew reassured her.

"I'll go upstairs and practice my lines." she said, heading upstairs, tears still trickling down her cheeks.

"She recites Shakespeare...I'm doing something right," Matthew said, "I'm gonna go upstairs and lay down."

"You do that," Rayna said, "I'll make a blueberry pie, and I'll fry up some steaks and potatoes."

"You're an angel." Matthew said, half-smiling.

"No, I'm a witch." Rayna replied, smirking.

For a brief minute, he swept her into his arms and kissed her with passion, wrapping his fingers in her hair.

"Go rest," she said, pulling away, "I'll call you when dinner is ready."

Matthew walked up the stairs and went in their bedroom, lying down and staring at the ceiling.

Matthew kept going over the past hour in his head. Lester didn't care about people – just profits. For a brief second, his eyes glowed red. But then he drifted to sleep, feeling at peace, listening to Rose recite the lines from the balcony scene.

* * *

Matthew sliced into his steak hard, imagining Lester's fat body being carved up.

"Um...sweetie...your eyes are red..." Rayna whispered, trembling a little but stroking his arm.

As he heard her voice and felt her touch, Matthew calmed down and his eyes returned to blue.

He looked at his steak and saw it shredded into jagged pieces, the rare meat dripping red juice on the plate.

"Sorry." he apologized, putting a piece in his mouth.

As he chewed, he thought about every report he got – nothing but praise and high recommendation for a promotion, which he never got. His teeth gnashed the meat between them, turning it to mush. As he swallowed, Rayna nudged him.

"You have me worried…" she whispered in his ear, trailing off.

"I'm okay," he said, forcing a half-smile.

"May I be excused?" Rose asked, "I don't feel very hungry." She was shaking.

"But you didn't finish -" Matthew began.

"Of course. Go do your homework." Rayna cut him off.

Rose ran up the stairs and slammed her bedroom door. Matthew put his head in his hands, running his fingers through his hair.

"Hon, you're…um…" Rayna started.

"I know." he growled.

Rayna took her empty plate, shaking like Rose did, as she washed it. After she put her silverware and plate in the drainer, she wrapped her arms around Matthew.

"Feel this." she murmured, placing her hand over his heart.

Matthew closed his eyes and felt her touch cooling his whole body, especially his heart. It felt like having a menthol pain killer on your skin. When his breathing eased, she lifted her hand.

"It's eight o'clock. Go to bed early. I'm gonna just watch some television, and then I'll be up." Rayna said, pulling him up and pushing him towards the stairs.

"Yes, dear." he replied, smiling.

As he walked upstairs and the bedroom door shut, Rayna turned on NBC and watched The Voice. She fell asleep as Adam blocked John Legend, lost in a cloud of dreams.

She woke up at 11pm. She saw the news. A building was burning in Salem.

"This was an organic grocery store – now a pile of ashes. The five alarm fire started at nine o'clock. One employee was killed. He stayed late into the evening and couldn't escape. The manager of the store identified the man as Lester Krause, saying he saw him before he left for the evening. Information to come on how the fire started." The young reporter announced.

Rayna's eyes went wide.

"No. It can't be...he wouldn't do this.." she muttered, pulling the blanket closer around her.

She closed her eyes, shivering, promising herself she would give him a chance to explain.

There was an explanation, she knew it. He wouldn't do this. Then she remembered his behavior at dinner.

Was it him?

She came back to him. He wouldn't betray that trust.

* * *

The next morning, Rayna traipsed down the stairs in her robe, opening the front door and bending over to get the paper. When she looked up she saw a faint trail of smoke in the air. Rayna shivered. She went inside, took the paper out of the plastic bag, and put it on the kitchen table.

The fire was the headline, to no surprise.

Rayna cracked a few eggs and scrambled them up. She would make a quiche. She had cheddar cheese and ham in the fridge. She would also toast bread with butter in the oven on the bottom rack.

'Maybe this will keep Matthew on an even keel.' she thought.

* * *

Matthew awoke and rubbed his eyes and face, looking at the clock.

"Jesus, yesterday hit me hard." he mumbled to himself.

"It must've..." Rayna trailed off, staring at him from the foot of the bed

"What's wrong?" he asked.

"How angry were you about losing your job?" she asked.

"I felt at peace last night. Why?"

She turned on the TV in their room and flipped it to the local news. Matthew saw the fire, and the name of the victim.

"I-I didn't do this..." he stuttered, getting up.

"You promise?" she asked, crossing her arms and coming closer to him.

"You trust me, right? And I've never done anything to break that trust?" he asked.

"Well, that's questionable." Rayna said, putting her hands on her hips.

Matthew pulled her into his lap and nuzzled her neck.

"Honey, I would never do anything to hurt you or anyone else," he paused, "Well maybe Samuel and his hoard."

Rayna chuckled.

"They have it coming." she admitted.

She stood up and pulled Matthew to his feet. Rayna put her arms around his neck and looked deep in his eyes.

"I love you. I know you didn't do this." she apologized, kissing him.

Nakiyah entered the house, wondering why Rayna wasn't at work yet. She was always at the store by seven, and it was now nine. She walked into the kitchen, smelling delicious food. The newspaper was on the kitchen table, along with the breakfast Rayna cooked.

She read the headline, and her eyes turned milky white. She stomped up the stairs and into the bedroom. Rayna sensed her presence and turned around. She released Matthew and stood between them. Matthew backed up a little.

"How could you do this?!" Nakiyah boomed.

"Look, take a breath and calm down..." Matthew said.

Nakiyah inhaled through her nose and exhaled a gust of wind, sending Matthew flying into the wall. Rayna stood steady, positioning herself in front of Matthew.

"Dammit, I didn't mean like that!" he exclaimed, clutching his neck.

"I trusted you with my niece! I trusted you with this town! And then this?! You haven't changed at all!" Nakiyah echoed again, little swirls of air twirling in her eyes.

"OK, go downstairs, drink some of your herbal tea, and we'll come down and talk!" Rayna boomed.

The shower turned on in the bedroom's bathroom, and Rayna rolled her eyes.

"I'm going to turn the faucet off. YOU go downstairs, and YOU get out of your pajamas and into clothes. I'm done with this shit." Rayna snapped, stomping into the bathroom.

Nakiyah's eyes went back to amber. She narrowed her eyes at Matthew before heading down to the kitchen. Matthew stood up gingerly, rubbing his knee. He took off his red silky pajamas and changed into an orange plaid button down shirt, jeans, and loafers. When Rayna came out of the bathroom, with wet hair, she took his hand.

"I'm sorry. She just - " Rayna began.

"She has every reason to have doubts. Look what happened in your family. We'll talk to her and figure this out." he reassured her.

They walked into the kitchen, hand in hand. Rayna got plates and silverware and set places at the table, putting out leaf-print fabric napkins. They all sat down with slowness, eyeing each other.

"You..." Nakiyah growled.

"You love quiche!" Rayna cut her off, "Here, have a slice!"

She put slices on Matthew and Nakiyah's plates, along with a piece of Italian bread with butter baked into it.

Matthew used his fork to cut off small pieces and he swallowed them with anxious gulps.

"You're a half-demon – you must still have urges!" Nakiyah insisted, "How am I supposed to trust you with anything anymore?!"

"Look, I swear, I didn't do this. Put me through any test you want – I didn't do this." Matthew promised, putting his hands together in a prayer position.

Nakiyah walked over to him. She put her thumbs over his eyes and closed hers. After a few minutes, she opened them and removed her hands.

"You didn't do this..." she trailed off, sitting back down and picking at her quiche.

"Ahem," Rayna cleared her throat, "Don't you have something to say to Matthew?"

"I'm sorry." Nakiyah muttered, biting into her bread.

"It's okay," Matthew replied, "I understand."

"No, you don't." Nakiyah insisted.

Matthew got tears in his eyes as he put his fork down.

"Samuel killed my wife." he admitted to her aunt for the first time.

Nakiyah looked up in shock.

"That was...your price?" she asked.

"Yeah. He took the love of my life from me, and now...he wants Rayna."

Nakiyah reached over and squeezed his shoulder.

"He won't get her." she insisted.

"So who did this?" Rayna asked.

"Well, it had to be someone with the same powers.." Nakiyah began, perching her head on her palm in thought.

Rayna took the newspaper and scanned the article for information.

"The cause of the fire was a gas leak – a faulty freezer sparked, and the store exploded in flames." she read aloud.

"Kyle isn't powerful enough..." Nakiyah said, then froze.

"What?" Rayna asked.

"It's him." Nakiyah stated, her fists clenching.

"Who?" Matthew asked.

"Samuel."

They all stood still at that moment staring into space in the kitchen, shocked.

"Let's...let's just eat this quiche and bread before they get cold..." Rayna stammered.

They ate in silence, all digesting more than breakfast.

Chapter Nineteen

Tiffany walked out of the cafe with her soy chai latte, dressed in a black short skirt and an orange polo shirt with the buttons undone to her cleavage, with black heeled boots on. The amethyst bracelet was on her wrist and a thin silver chain with a jeweled infinity symbol graced her neck.

Tiffany entered *Midnight Tomes* and saw a curvy caramel-toned woman with blue eyes and curly brown hair standing at the register. The woman looked up at the sound of the bell and gazed at her.

"Can I help you with anything?" she asked.

"Yeah, I'm looking for the woman that gave me this." Tiffany replied, showing her the bracelet.

"Nakiyah!" Rayna called.

Tiffany stared at the floor and swayed a bit, smoothing out her skirt.

"You seem...different than most." Rayna said, an eyebrow raised.

"Um...I'm certainly unique." Tiffany brushed off.

As Nakiyah came to the front, she saw Tiffany and froze. It was the half-demon she gave protection and strength.

"Did...the bracelet work?" she asked, backing up behind the counter.

"Yes, it brought me to a safe place...where I met someone." Tiffany answered.

"Someone you love?" Nakiyah asked.

Rayna looked from one to the other, curious.

"Yeah, more than anything. We have unfinished business – so we came back." she explained.

Nakiyah walked past her and put up the 'closed' sign on the door.

"I know what you are. I knew when I met you," Nakiyah stated, a tight line in her lips, "Now you're back. What do you want?"

"Then why did you help me?" Tiffany asked.

"Because...I can't turn down any being in need." Nakiyah admitted.

"I need to know if you have something to help me." Tiffany admitted.

"Like what?"

"Um, I'm not sure..." Tiffany trailed off.

Nakiyah came closer to her, standing within an inch of her. She stared into her eyes, narrowing hers. She felt a pull. She stroked Tiffany's hair and face.

"No!" she exclaimed, backing away.

"Oh God..." Tiffany turned away, her head in her hands.

"That's what he gave you." Nakiyah replied, still shaking.

"How do I -" she began.

"Destroy them?" Rayna asked.

"Yeah," Tiffany said, with a furrowed brow.

"Those monsters will indulge in your guilt. It will foil everything, and they will be stronger for it." Rayna explained.

"All I can tell you is they gather at the full moon, which is tonight. They will be in a clearing in the forest surrounded by rocks and candles." Nakiyah gulped, taking out a protection candle and making the sign of the pentacle over it, whispering something.

"What are you doing?" Tiffany asked.

"You need to go tonight with your lover. You will need back-up." Nakiyah deflected.

"Will...he...be there?" Tiffany asked, trembling.

"All ceremonial work is done at midnight." Nakiyah replied.

"Thank you both." Tiffany said, taking a deep breath.

Nakiyah looked deep into her eyes.

"You can do this. I know it."

Tiffany half-smiled and left, the door clanging shut.

"They're going to join us, aren't they?" Rayna asked Nakiyah.

"I sense they will. And they'll be dedicated."

"But it won't be just the four corners anymore. What will it be?" Rayna asked.

"Six of Salem. Our coven."

* * *

Tiffany walked through the woods in silver sandals with a lace purple dress on – and a push-up bra to amplify her breasts. She saw the clearing ahead.

Tiffany closed her eyes and focused on her power. When she opened them, they glowed purple.

As she entered the clearing, she saw men in various outfits – a guy who looked like someone from a death metal band, a guy wearing a flannel shirt and jeans, someone wearing a blue collar worker's shirt with his name embroidered and black pants.

There were ten of them.

"Whoa, she's one of us, guys." the singer said, looking at her.

"Did you come to join us?" the blue collar worker asked.

"I came to bless you all with my gifts." She husked walking up to him, and stroking his chest, rubbing his package.

"Lord Below..." he moaned, as she kept rubbing.

She felt his life force entering her. Her eyes glowed brighter.

"Yes..." she enticed, kissing him.

As he climaxed, his eyes opened wide and he fell to the ground, motionless.

"Kill her!" the flannel guy shouted.

They surrounded her, holding their hands up, their eyes bright red. Tiffany trembled, her eyes going back to normal.

"Stop!" a voice yelled.

They looked away, distracted. They saw Marina, her long curly brown hair blowing in a sudden wind, thunder cracking above as she raised her hands. Lightning flashed, and rain poured down.

"Do it!" Marina shouted.

"Do what?" Tiffany asked, still shaken.

"Get angry! Now!"

Tiffany saw them closing in on Marina, their eyes glowing red again. Tiffany's eyes lit up purple. A swift wind of jasmine blew towards Marina. The men followed it like zombies drawn to brains. As they circled her, Marina aimed her hands at the sky. Lightning came striking down. It entered all ten of their bodies, frying them like breaded cod. They fell to the ground, their bodies smoking and black in spots.

Down in the bowels of Hell, Samuel doubled over, screaming in pain, almost falling into the river of lava. Another sub-demon pulled him up.

"My men...they're dead..." Samuel croaked.

"Better not let the boss know." the sub-demon chuckled.

"DON'T YOU LAUGH AT ME!" Samuel roared, standing to full height.

The sub-demon cowered, trembling.

"I'll take care of this." Samuel growled, disappearing in a burst of flame.

Tiffany and Marina collapsed on the ground, zapped of strength by the sheer force. Marina crawled over to Tiffany and tried to hug her.

"Ride the lightning, baby." she said, smiling.

A flash of fire struck in front of them...

...and Samuel appeared.

"You whores!" he boomed. "No one crosses me!"

He aimed his hands up at them and formed a fireball in his hand.

"You...won't....hurt...us..." Marina growled.

She aimed her hands towards the sky, and lightning struck Samuel, electrocuting him. He fell to the ground stunned. Marina's eyes closed, passing out.

"I'll get you out of here, babe." Tiffany said, picking Marina up in her arms and carrying her through the woods to their car on the deserted road, while Samuel twitched on the ground.

As they drove away, he stumbled to a standing position his eyes glowing red.

"Oh there are more of us," he laughed in a booming tone.

"Many more."

* * *

Tiffany nudged open the apartment door and laid Marina on the soft baby blue couch. She was still out cold. She sat her up and tapped her cheek a few times. Her eyes rolled open, unable to focus.

"Where...where am I?" Marina mumbled.

"You're home. You need to replenish yourself." Tiffany said.

"Baby, no." Marina refused.

"Just breathe in." Tiffany ordered, opening Marina's mouth and placing hers over it.

Tiffany took in a deep breath and exhaled into Marina's mouth. She felt Tiffany's life force and power flowing into her. She felt her strength coming back – no longer trembling or tired. She pulled away when she felt she had enough.

"You can't kill me. Remember that." Tiffany said, kissing her with gentleness.

"Is he - " Marina began.

"No. He was knocked out for a while. Long enough for us to leave."

Marina sat up and pulled the blanket around her from the back of the couch, shivering.

"Can you put the heat on?" Marina asked.

"Shit. This did wear you down." Tiffany replied, turning up the thermostat.

Marina wrapped her arms around herself, getting chills. Tiffany went into the kitchen and made her a cup of rose hip and bergamot tea. She squeezed some honey into it, some lemon juice, and added a packet of sweetener. She stirred it up and walked back into the main area, handing it to Marina.

"This will comfort you and relax you." Tiffany explained.

"I'm kinda hungry. Do we have any muffins left from baking this morning?" Marina asked.

"Yes, I'll get us both one. I'm famished too."

As she went into the kitchen to get the muffins, the phone rang. Tiffany looked at the caller ID and her eyes widened. She shivered uncontrollably. Marina was recovering, so she forced herself under control.

"Who was that?" Marina asked.

"I checked the voice mail – just a robo call." Tiffany lied.

As they ate their muffins, there was a knock on the door. Tiffany just sipped her tea and nibbled her muffin. She knew that putrid, hot energy anywhere.

"Shouldn't we answer that?" Marina asked.

"No, I don't think so." Tiffany insisted.

"Come on. We can't leave whoever it is standing there."

Marina trudged to the door and began to open it.

"NO!" Tiffany yelled.

A blast of energy threw Marina to the floor, leaving her writhing on the floor.

"Hey, bitch. You should learn to hide better." a menacing voice said.

"K-Kyle..." Tiffany stammered.

She stumbled off the couch and backed into the kitchen, Kyle advancing on her.

"Did you forget the welts? The bruises? The broken bones? Or how I promised I'd burn you to ashes if you ever left?" he growled, clenching his fists.

"You – you can't hurt me..." she stuttered, backing into the oven.

"Oh yes I can. Just like I broke your lover in half."

"Oh you will pay. Dearly. You will watch me kill her. You will watch as I burn her one body part at a time – until she is screaming for mercy...but there will be none – "

"Oh baby...do we have to fight? I'm back now." she husked, running her hands through his hair.

"Don't - " he began.

"Don't what? Please you?" she whispered, nibbling on his earlobe.

He closed his eyes and moaned before pulling away.

"You slut! You can't fool me!" he shouted.

"Fuck me," she whispered, "Fuck that whore out of me."

Tiffany looked deep into his eyes, opening his shirt and running her tongue up and down his chest.

"I'm gonna fuck you til you realize where you belong." he growled.

Tiffany saw Marina getting up from behind Kyle and winked at her. As Kyle undid his pants and began to fuck her on the counter, hard and fast, getting closer to climax, Tiffany kissed him deeply, her tongue stroking his mouth – and she had to fight back a gagging sound. She felt like throwing up, but it was a sacrifice.

As he came and his life force flew into her, Marina aimed her hands at him, and electricity flew from her fingers into him. He convulsed, his eyes rolling back into his head, stumbling backwards with and falling back on the floor. As she continued to electrocute him, he choked out, "You...little...witch..."

"I'd rather be one of them, than one of you." Tiffany spat, pushing him to the floor.

He burst into flames from the trio of powers, burning into a pile of ashes.

"I need to get in a shower and get him off me." Tiffany said, choking on a gag.

"I'll get you clean." Marina said, leading her into the bathroom.

Marina filled the tub with hot water and bubble bath. She helped Tiffany off with her clothes and into the tub. She gently scrubbed at her skin with a shower puff, the creamy body wash foaming on her skin and replacing the burnt, venomous smell of sex with an evil half-demon to lilies and gardenia – any trace of him removed. She washed her hair with her favorite shampoo and rinsed her off with the shower head.

Marina wrapped Tiffany in a towel and brought her into the bedroom, drying her off and placing the towel in the hamper. Marina stood in front of her, love burning silver in her eyes.

"You'e so...beautiful." she murmured.

"Babe, I can't." Tiffany said, sniffling.

"I understand. I just wanted to make sure you knew how I see you." Marina whispered.

She dressed them both in pajamas and pulled Tiffany into bed, wrapping her arms around her.

"One down." Tiffany murmured.

"One to go." Marina finished.

Marina kissed her with depth and passion, before Tiffany pulled away.

"We need them." Tiffany said, a thought coming out of the blue.

"And they need us." Marina added.

"Midnight Tomes." Tiffany said.

"Tomorrow." Marina agreed.

As they curled up together, Marina smiled and kissed Tiffany's neck.

Maybe they could end this...

...once and for all.

Chapter Twenty

Tiffany entered *Midnight Tomes* with Marina. Rayna was pricing bags of white sage.

"Well...how did it turn out?" she asked.

"We took them out, and..." Tiffany trailed off.

"We fried the asshole." Marina finished, a silver glow in her eyes.

"Calm, babe." Tiffany coaxed.

Marina's eyes returned to blue.

"Look, we want to join your coven. Samuel deserves to burn in hell for the rest of eternity." Marina said with a steel tone to her voice.

"Nakiyah!" Rayna called.

She walked over to the door and turned it to 'Closed' and drew the shades. Nakiyah walked to the front, her braids hanging loose down her back.

"I see you finished ALL of them off." Nakiyah said, looking into their eyes, "And you want to join us. However, you haven't proven yourselves trustworthy."

"That's not possible. We killed ten half-demons and finished off the second in command." Tiffany argued.

"If you were really pure inside, you'd be immune to our powers." Nakiyah replied.

"Test us." Marina challenged, "I guarantee you we'd prove ourselves."

"You asked for it." Nakiyah said, raising her hands above her head.

"No!" Rayna said, "What if they die?"

"Then they weren't on our side." Nakiyah spat, "Now channel your powers."

Rayna closed her eyes for a minute, then opened them, blue sparking red. They aimed their hands at Marina and Tiffany. Rayna's blue and red sparks went into them and Nakiyah's wind power pushed at them. They stood steady. Rayna and Nakiyah squinted their eyes shut, shooting all possible power at them.

But they didn't move.

Nakiyah and Rayna collapsed on the ground, heaving breath.

"I...guess...I...was...wrong..." Nakiyah choked, gasping for air.

"I figured it out long ago. No half-demon would come to us for protection if they were under Samuel's control." Rayna said, leaning against the counter.

"You've proven yourselves," Nakiyah concluded, "You would've been demolished by our powers with no trace left."

Tiffany reached into her backpack and handed them two bottles of water. They drank with eagerness, gulping it down. Once they recovered, Rayna got up and scribbled something down on a piece of paper.

"Tomorrow is October 29. We have one day to prepare, and then the battle. On Halloween. They will be targeting the festival in town. We are the only ones who can save Salem."

Tiffany looked at the paper as Rayna handed it to her.

"What is this?" she asked.

"The address of my boyfriend's house. We are safe there." Rayna explained.

"Are you sure?" Marina asked.

"Even if something does happen...there's six of us. Samuel would come on his own to seek vengeance." Nakiyah replied.

"We'll be there." Marina and Tiffany said together, holding hands.

Nakiyah smiled at them.

"I'm glad you found each other. You pair well." she said, touching both of their arms.

Tiffany and Marina exited the bookstore.

"Are you sure this will work?" Tiffany asked.

"Sweetie, I want this over with – for us and for them. It will happen....

...I just know it."

* * *

Matthew walked into the circle surrounded by stones. He saw several black burn marks on the dirt.

"I know you're here, you bastard!" he yelled, "Face me like the man you were!"

Nothing happened.

"Get out here!" he screamed, "I want to see you NOW!"

The candles lit, and the bonfire in the middle lit. A burst of fire appeared in front of the circle, and there he was. Except he was different.

His skin was ragged on his face, revealing his skull and the bone of his facial structure. His clothes were centuries old pants and a white button-down shirt – torn and weathered. His feet left flaming footprints on the ground as he walked over to Matthew.

"This is who I am. Beneath the facade. This is what comes of dwelling in Hell for centuries." he cackled.

"Jesus Christ..." Matthew muttered, stepping back as Samuel reached out a half-fleshed hand.

"I made the fire to get even for you. That's what I wanted all these years for myself. She paid dearly, and so will everyone else." Samuel growled, his empty eye sockets burning with fire.

"I didn't want revenge." Matthew insisted.

"Don't be stupid. You wanted justice." Samuel countered, tapping his fingers together.

"Maybe at first. The woman you want to kill trusted me many times with her life. I may have weakened, but I won't break that promise. I remembered what was important...unlike you." Matthew said, tears stinging his eyes.

"I knew what was important!" Samuel roared, the flames of the bonfire shooting towards the sky.

"Did you forget how her arms felt around you? What it was like to kiss her?" Matthew asked with softness.

Samuel stared at the ground, the flames in his eyes disappearing for a minute. Tears sprang from the bone.

"She scorned me...she didn't want me." He clutched his rib cage, groaning in pain.

Fire returned to his eyes, and he stood upright.

"That's why Rayna must die. She is a reminder of pain and loss. Her face – her eyes – her smile – are all reminders. I will not be tortured by her anymore." he spat, "You will watch her die, or she will watch you die."

"I almost feel sorry for you..." Matthew trailed off, "...you will be sent back down to the bowels of misery you chose for yourself. And you will spend your eternity in pain, – wishing for Tituba. And you will never get out." Matthew finished.

He raised his hands and rain began to fall, putting out the bonfire and candles.

"What the hell?!" Samuel cursed.

"Rayna and I bonded. And you can't take that away from us. Or our powers." Matthew smirked.

"Good luck, you evil asshole." he snapped, walking out of the circle.

Samuel's jaw was agape. They had a chance. He had to fix things somehow.

There were two new girls. He smirked. They'd respond to one thing.

Pain.

* * *

Tiffany and Marina rang the doorbell. Rayna opened the door and ushered them in, hugging them.

"Have a seat." she offered, showing them a loveseat.

They sat down, hands intertwined, hoping this went well.

"Ah, you're here." Nakiyah said, walking in with a plate of cookies and some tea, "We're just waiting for Matthew and Rose. Then we will begin."

"Who are they?" Marina asked.

"My boyfriend and his daughter. They're part of the coven too." Rayna explained.

As they nibbled on cookies and sipped some of the rose hip and chamomile tea Nakiyah made, the door opened.

"We're here..." Matthew trailed off, looking at Marina and Tiffany, "WOAH!"

"Baby, calm down. They're okay."

"They're half-demons!" he exclaimed, putting himself in front of Rose.

Rose came out from behind her dad and walked towards them. He grabbed her hand, trying to pull her back, but she yanked away. She looked in their eyes and touched their hands.

"They're fine, Dad." she said.

"What do you mean, 'They're fine'?!" he exclaimed.

"I saw what they did."

As Rose told them what happened, Tiffany squeezed her eyes shut. She felt the men surrounding her – Kyle's body against hers – Samuel appearing and threatening them. She began shivering. Marina turned and saw her reaction.

"It's okay, it's over." she reassured her, rubbing her back and kissing her forehead.

"Okay, so she's...traumatized...and they destroyed some of Samuel's demons. But how can we trust them?" Matthew asked.

"Same way I trust you." Nakiyah said, narrowing her eyes.

"Touche." Matthew murmured.

"Look, let's get down to business. Nakiyah saw them destroying Salem on Halloween at the festival. We have to have a plan in place and train tomorrow." Rayna said.

"I already set up a training area hidden deep in the woods," Nakiyah added, "It's somewhere no one will see."

"How deep in the woods is it?" Matthew asked.

"Five miles. No one will think to hike or hunt that far."

"Now, for the battle. We need all the help we can get. Marina and Tiffany add a substantial Ace to our deck because their powers rivaled Kyle's – enough to kill him." Rayna began.

"And we cover the four corners, plus Rayna and I have bonded powers." Matthew added.

"I will try my hardest to keep up with all of you. I'm powerful, but not as much as the five of you." Nakiyah said.

"What can I do?" Rose asked.

"Since you control the earth, any kind of resistance for them is helpful." Matthew told his daughter.

"If Tiffany combines her power with mine, we can take out a good number of them. We took out ten – maybe with training we can take out more." Marina suggested.

"Just promise me I won't have to -" Tiffany began.

"No sex will be needed," Nakiyah told her, "Just use enough of your allure."

Rose grabbed a cookie and gobbled it down. Matthew looked at her and saw her trembling.

"Honey, it will all be over in two days. Then we can go back to nor-mal...whatever normal is now." he said, hugging her.

Tiffany and Marina froze. They heard a voice.

Not all of them trust you. They will get what they want and kill you. They know you're like the rest of us. Come with me and be safe. I will pro-tect you.

"Did you hear that?" Tiffany whispered.

"Yeah. I'm ignoring it." Marina whispered back.

"What if he's right?" Tiffany asked.

"He's not. Don't let him trick you." Marina whispered, stroking her hand.

They heard rustling outside. Rayna looked out the door and saw nothing. She sat back down on the couch with Nakiyah.

As they talked, Samuel peered in the bay window. He watched the way the moonlight hit Rayna's face. He looked at her curvy frame.

He closed his eyes.

Samuel felt Tituba's silky skin caressing his, her gentle kisses, her nails down his back, her amber eyes looking into his. How he felt his soul join with hers as they climaxed.

Then he remembered the way she turned her back on him. Banned him from the shack.

Fire lit in his eyes.

"They will pay. And since those two new witches won't listen, I'll have to do my worst." he hissed.

"Did you hear something?" Rayna asked.

"Yeah...sounded like a familiar voice." Matthew said, narrowing his eyes and looking out the window.

He saw nothing.

"I think it was him." he said.

"Babe, there was no one out there."

"He comes and goes at will! How easy would it be for him to spy on us and then disappear?" Matthew asked.

Suddenly, a burst of fire appeared in the middle of the living room. Samuel appeared, in his classic black pinstripe suit with red tie, black hair slicked back, shiny dress shoes on.

"Well, well, well – a meeting of the heathens."

He approached Tiffany and Marina.

"You both escaped my grasp before, but I have a way to change your mind." he said, chuckling.

"We would never - "

Samuel reached out and grabbed Rayna, twisting her fingers. She screamed in pain.

"Just say yes and this all will stop." Samuel coaxed, bending them back, "She won't feel anymore pain."

"How do we know you won't kill her?!" Tiffany asked.

Matthew grabbed Samuel by the neck and twisted it, attempting to snap it in half, but all it did was snap backwards. Samuel grinned at him upside down.

"HOLY SHIT!" he screamed, flying back against the staircase.

"I'm dead, asshole!" Samuel cackled.

He snapped his head forward and adjusted it. He held a small ball of fire in his hand. He held it over Rayna's head, grinning with sharp teeth.

"I can turn over my hand, and she'll be gone. Make your choice." he growled.

Marina lunged after him. The fireball flew at Marina, but she shot a bolt of lightning at it, evaporating it. He used her distance to grab her and twist her arm in an awkward direction. She screamed in pain.

"Well, Tiffany, are you in?" he asked, a red glow in his eyes.

Tiffany began to weep.

"Don't...do it..." Marina cried out.

Rose's eyes glowed amber.

"You messed with the wrong family." she spat.

She raised her hands and vines with thick, petrified stems wrapped around him, Marina pulling free and crawling over to Tiffany. At that moment, Rayna, Matthew, and Nakiyah raised their arms and shot out electric power into him – Rayna and Matthew's red and blue, Nakiyah's a white beam. He screamed in pain. When it seemed he couldn't move anymore, Rose wove her hands and removed the vines, and the other three stopped. He writhed on the floor, moaning in pain.

"This is just a taste," Nakiyah said, stepping on his crotch, causing him to cry out more, "You have no idea what you're in for."

Matthew and Rayna picked him up and threw him out the door, closing it and locking it.

Samuel brought himself up to a kneeling position, breathing heavy, lacerating pain still going through his body.

"You...will...pay..." he gasped, disappearing in a burst of flame.

He appeared down in Hell, collapsing into his ember chair, every bit of his demon energy wasted. He heard thundering footsteps approaching.

"You let them defeat you?!" the deep voice boomed.

"I was outnumbered...I wasn't aware..." Samuel began.

"Their power has been growing!! Now they have two of ours in their coven!! And Kyle is dead!!" the demon yelled.

"I am trying my hard-"

"NO YOU'RE NOT!" the demon screamed.

"We will get them. I will bring my hoard, and we will destroy the Six of Salem. Hell and Earth shall be one." Samuel promised.

"It better. Or else..." The demon trailed off, looking to the side.

Samuel looked an saw the giant cauldron of lava with bones sticking out.

He gulped hard.

He needed to win.

He needed them all dead.

Chapter Twenty One

Marina and Tiffany trailed behind Rose in the line of their coven, walking through the woods, leaves crunching under their feet. The sun was just rising, when people wouldn't be awake. They were almost five miles out from any road or house, no path leading back to them. The smell of maple and oak was in the air, invigorating the six of them.

They approached a clearing with a bubbling brook running next to it. A few ducks and some white geese paddled by them.

"This feels so peaceful." Marina said, taking a deep breath and exhaling.

"I come here on weekends," Nakiyah said, stroking the bark of an oak tree, "It calms me and I seem to soak in the power from the surroundings."

"So this is why you chose it." Rayna surmised.

"Yes. He will do anything he can to destroy all of us. I brought sandbags for Marina and Tiffany, Rose can practice on me, and you & Matthew can practice on the scarecrows I bought from a dollar shop." Nakiyah directed.

Tiffany walked Marina & Tiffany over to the sandbags.

"Tiffany, we know you are alluring. However, Marina needs to work on her powers. You can destroy these twenty sandbags – right down into nothing." Nakiyah informed them.

"I'll try." Marina said.

"No, you will do it. Trust me." Nakiyah countered.

Marina's lightning started to fly into the sandbag, but the sparks fizzled out. Her shoulders slumped. Tiffany walked over and looked her in the eye.

"You're letting your nerves get to you. Feel your anger."

"I don't want to imagine the past few days." Marina argued.

"No. Close your eyes and envision something else." Tiffany said with softness.

Marina rolled her eyes and closed them.

"Imagine us in that street. Surrounded by half-demons. They move in closer and closer. We are outnumbered. Five of them surround you and me. And the only way you can save me is by using your power. One of the demons grabs my wrist, and my skin starts to burn - "

Marina opened her eyes, and they were silver. She aimed her hands at the sandbag, her teeth bared, and she shot her lightning into it, the heat surrounding all of them. She zapped each sandbag – one by one – until they all were gone.

As her eyes went back to normal, Tiffany wrapped her arms around Marina's neck and kissed her with passion.

"Not here babe," Marina whispered, "Later."

"No canoodling!" Rose yelled from where she was.

They chuckled and walked over to where she was.

"You do vine work very well," Nakiyah praised Rose, "Now I want you to try to use your powers in other ways."

"How ?" Rose asked.

Nakiyah stood four feet away from her.

"Try to stop my powers. However you can imagine it." she ordered.

She swirled her hands around, whipping up some winds, and shot them at Rose. Rose started to slide back, and she fell, landing on her rear. Nakiyah stopped and helped her up.

"I know you're not good under pressure, but use your imagination." Nakiyah chided.

She resumed her distance and again created the winds, pushing them against Rose. Rose struggled to keep her footing.

"Imagine Nakiyah getting mad at your father and using her powers on him!" Rayna yelled.

Rose closed her eyes and saw Nakiyah whipping her father up in tornado force winds and tossing him against a tree. When she opened them, they were glowing amber. She rose her hands up and dirt formed walls on either side of Nakiyah. Before they could collapse on her, she ran out of the way, the soil forming a mountain where she was standing.

"Very good." Nakiyah praised.

Rayna and Matthew shot red and blue intertwined bolts into the scarecrows, burning them until they disappeared. When Matthew looked back at Rose, his bolts died off.

"Babe, you can't keep your eye on Rose. It will be you, me, and Nakiyah versus Samuel. Marina, Tiffany, and Rose will be destroying the rest of the half-demons." Rayna explained, stroking his arm.

"I know...I just worry about her." Matthew grumbled, running a hand through his hair.

"Look at that display of strength Rose just created!" Rose exclaimed, motioning back to her, where she was currently felling small trees and bushes, ripping them from the ground with her power and tossing them through the air.

"She cracked a huge tree at the school a few weeks ago!" Rayna added.

"Ok, let's try again." he agreed, looking at the remaining ten scarecrows.

He closed his eyes and imagined Samuel going after Rose for revenge. He opened them, and they were red, sparking blue. Rayna closed her eyes and imagined Samuel setting Nakiyah on fire, her screams echoing in the empty streets. She opened her eyes and they aimed their hands at the ten scarecrows and, one by one, demolished them in seconds flat.

Nakiyah, Marina, Tiffany, and Rose walked over to them.

"I think we are ready." Nakiyah said.

"If we rely on our emotions, we have a chance." Rayna agreed.

"I don't know how many he will have – or what he will do to get to us – it's all fuzzy." Nakiyah admitted.

"All we can do is our best." Rose said.

"If that's enough..." Tiffany trailed off.

"I want you all to burn protection candles tonight. We will go back to the store now and get them. They will keep us safe tonight." Nakiyah added.

"Let's go..." Rayna said, shivering, "I feel a chill in the wind."

"Here, babe." Matthew said, putting his coat on her shoulders.

They walked back through the woods the way they came, each one with a seed of doubt in their mind. It took concerted effort to conjure their power. None of them said the word 'fail' to Nakiyah. Their heads would be bitten off in a second.

Nakiyah trembled and pulled her sweater around her.

She was first on Samuel's list. She knew it.

She let the next in the bloodline survive 33 years ago.

* * *

Samuel paced the circle where his minions gathered, mumbling to himself. The other half-demons watched with discomfort. Their master was upset. They waited for him to say something, until one spoke up.

"Um, are you going to give us any directions?" a guy in flannel and jeans with red eyes asked.

Samuel glared at him, the red in his eyes flaring.

The guy backed up and stumbled, falling on the forest floor.

Samuel cleared his throat and stood at the front of the circle.

"You all know what we are to do tomorrow. We must destroy every human being at that festival tomorrow. Then we must destroy any living relative of Tituba – plus the rest of the Six of Salem. Then Salem will be in ruins. Only we will survive. Only we can save them..." he trailed off, cackling.

"By making them like us!!!" he boomed, raising his hands to the sky and bursting into a cacophony of Hellish sounds.

"Soon our kind will rule the earth – little by little. It will be our paradise." he said in a softer tone, grinning with his jagged teeth.

All the men and women in the circle smiled with satisfaction.

"A monarchy." a woman in a grey business suit said, rubbing her hands together.

"A fiery Hell on earth." a guy dressed in a football jersey and sweatpants hissed.

"Now...we summon him. We call to our true master." Samuel said, raising his arms to the air.

The rest of them did the same – about twenty of them – chanting in a strange language, the bonfire blazing higher and higher. Suddenly the winds whipped up and thunder cracked. Where it struck on the ground, the head demon appeared.

"So – you are preparing for battle." he said in a scratchy tone.

"Yes, master. I have rallied and excited our kind. Soon we will rule Salem." Samuel said, bowing to him.

"You aren't aware of what happened today." the head demon commented.

Samuel looked up, alarmed.

"What happened today?" he asked.

"...they know." the demon said.

"What?! How is that possible?!" Samuel exclaimed.

"The older one has vision. And the younger one has seen what will happen. You are ill prepared. They spent all day training for battle. And they will be there tomorrow." the demon said, smirking.

"THOSE GODDAMN WITCHES!" Samuel screamed.

The entire group jumped a little.

"Then do something about it." the demon said, "You know what awaits you if you don't."

Samuel gulped and remembered the small demons carrying the bowl of demonic soup to the Highest of Hell.

"I WILL succeed," he insisted, "I don't care how many we lose!"

"Woah!" one half-demon exclaimed, dressed in a red dress and black boots, "You don't give a shit about us?!"

"YOU ARE EXPENDABLE!" The head demon screamed, moving into the circle.

The half-demons all backed away, shaking, nodding to his statement.

"Good. Now that's settled, Samuel – I am doing something I have never done before." the head demon said, approaching him.

"...what?" Samuel asked, taking a step back.

"Helping you." the head demon grinned, placing his hand on his forehead.

Samuel felt heat racing through him. He screamed at the heat, collapsing on the ground. The rest of the demons screamed as well, some falling to their knees and arching their backs, some falling onto the grass.

"What...the...hell...was...that..." he gasped.

"All of you – your fire power is ten times more effective. I expect to see many deaths tomorrow. There is no way you can fail now." the head demon informed him, "And now I take my leave. Do the Highest of Hell's bidding."

He disappeared in a huge blast of fire, leaving burn marks on the ground.

"Well, well, well...." Samuel began, laughing.

"They will never survive."

* * *

Rayna lit the last protection candle – on the kitchen table where they were having dinner. Matthew made a pot roast with carrots, potatoes, and celery in the slow cooker, baked a loaf of cornbread and a pumpkin pie.

Rose pushed her vegetables and meat around on her plate, leaning her elbow on the table and resting her chin in her hand. Rayna took small pieces up on her fork and chewed them. Matthew cut up his potato with a slow sawing motion.

It was silent.

"Dad, Rayna..." Rose began.

They both looked up.

"What if I die tomorrow?" she asked, a tear sliding down her cheek.

Her father and Rayna came over and hugged her.

"We would never let that happen." Rayna said.

"What if I lose one of you?" Rose asked, sniffling.

"Look, we can't guarantee tomorrow. You're old enough to understand that tomorrow is never a given – you're 18, going on 19. You're starting college next fall. Instead of mulling over death, cherish today." Matthew said.

"Your father is right. We have a delicious meal he cooked, we're together – with this candle to protect us. We trained all morning today. That's the most we can do. Besides, Samuel doesn't want you..he wants...me." Rayna said, looking down.

Matthew tipped her chin up and looked in her eyes.

"I will never let him harm you. I don't care what it takes – I will destroy him. He's not going to take two women I love away from me." Matthew said with firmness, kissing her.

"I don't want you giving your life for me." Rayna said, a tear sliding down her own cheek.

"We will both do our best to survive," he replied, "and we will make the Six of Salem survive."

"And save the town." Rose added.

"Yeah...I've lived here my whole life. This town went through enough – it's time for someone to stop the madness." Rayna stated in a voice edged with steel.

"Come on," Matthew chided them, "Let's finish this dinner so we can have that pumpkin pie."

He smiled at Rayna and Rose, and they smiled back. They ate with enthusiasm, making sounds at the deliciousness of the food and going back to talking about school & life at Midnight Tomes.

As he cut and served the slices of pie – with whipped cream sprinkled with pumpkin spice & brown sugar – Matthew grimaced when they couldn't see him.

Everything was on the line tomorrow.

He knew it was up to him to protect Rayna & Rose.

Chapter Twenty Two

It was four o'clock AM. Marina stepped outside the door of their apartment building in her pajamas and bare feet. There was a briskness to the air, and the sun was starting to come out.

"I can fix that." she whispered.

She raised her arms to the sky, her eyes glowing silver. Clouds gathered in the sky, thunder struck, and rain poured down.

"Rain come down and hit the streets
Where the witches and demons shall meet
Pour down your goodness before wrong is made right
'Til the hour strikes midnight.
So mote it be."

She winked at the sky and went back up the stairs to their apartment, her clothes soaked. When she got inside, Tiffany had a black long-sleeve thermal shirt, sweatpants, and fleece socks out for her.

"Thanks babe." Marina said, changing with quickness, shivering from the weather she created.

"I have one more thing for you." Tiffany said, reaching into a velvet drawstring bag.

She attached a sterling silver chain around Marina's neck with a diamond lightning bolt hanging from it.

"Thank you." Marina murmured, kissing her.

"Nakiyah says when night falls, she'll meet all of us in front of her house, and we'll walk to *Midnight Tomes*. She saw Samuel's group gathering at the square nearby. They will see the rain and know we did it." Tiffany explained to her.

"Let's hope for the best." Marina said, hugging her.

"I love you." Tiffany said, with tears in her eyes.

"I love you too." Marina breathed in her ear.

* * *

As dusk started to fall, Rayna was slipping on an army green hoodie. Matthew walked out of the bathroom in a black pullover sweatshirt and jeans. They both exchanged strained looks.

"I guess this is it." Rayna murmured.

"Yeah...this is our chance." Matthew agreed.

Rayna slipped her pentacle necklace on.

"How is Rose doing?" she asked, wincing.

"She jumps at every sound and touch," Matthew replied, "We have to be strong for her."

"She needs to be strong for herself." Rayna reminded him.

He nodded.

"Let's go get her." Matthew said, letting out a shaky exhale.

"Yeah. Nakiyah will be waiting."

They knocked on Rose's door, and she emerged wearing a hippie-style brown blouse with flowers embroidered on it.

"Can we have a minute, babe?" Rayna asked Matthew.

"Sure. I'll go get our jackets." he agreed, traipsing down the stairs.

Rayna looked Rose in her eyes and grasped her shoulders.

"Look, I know this is scary, but do you remember when you stoood up to Kyle? He found you in the woods and tried to attack you." Rayna reminded her.

"Yeah..." Rose trailed off.

"Well, do you also remember how you used your powers to keep him from doing anything to you? That was what a strong woman does! She doesn't let anyone hurt her – and if they do, she doesn't let them take any part of her with them." Rayna explained.

"I get it. I just worry." Rose replied, wringing her hands.

"You have to use whatever fuels your emotions to get you through this. If it helps, think of me and your dad fighting! You have your father's strength, and you developed my quick-thinking. You CAN do this." she encouraged Rose, hugging her.

"Thanks, Rayna." Rose said, hugging her back.

"Well, let's not keep Nakiyah waiting. We have some demons to destroy." Rayna said, smiling.

They walked down the stairs, ready to face whatever was going to be thrown at them.

* * *

Nakiyah was waiting where she said she would, Marina and Tiffany already standing by her. The stars started to shine, and the full moon hung in the sky.

"Halloween was cancelled due to the weather and rescheduled for the next day – even though the rain stopped five minutes ago." Nakiyah said, smiling at Marina.

Marina smiled back.

"Mysteriously enough, everyone is in a deep sleep. I wonder who did that..." Rayna trailed off, smirking.

"Come on, time to go." Nakiyah ordered, smiling despite her stern tone.

They walked in a line down the streets to *Midnight Tomes*. When they reached the square, they formed a circle around it, facing outward in the corners of the brick border around the fountain.

Then, they saw them – Samuel leading a hoard of half-demons, all with red eyes and heat radiating from their hands.

Nakiyah glanced at all the members of the Six of Salem.

"We're ready." Tiffany answered for the group.

Nakiyah smiled and turned to face Samuel. Her eyes were milky white.

"So, the sinners prepared." Samuel growled, facing them with twenty demons behind him.

"I'd look in the mirror, you bastard." Rayna hissed, her eyes glowing blue with red sparks.

"Sorry, I break mirrors when I look in them." he laughed.

"That's not something to brag about." Matthew said with a smirk.

"Ah, one of the traitors – the one I helped the most by relieving his wife of her pain." Samuel remarked, tapping his fingers together.

"YOU ASSHOLE! YOU BURNED HER ALIVE!" Matthew roared, leaping at him, Rayna and Nakiyah holding him back.

"As I did to many other casualties in the past few centuries, empowered by the damned." Samuel grinned with his jagged teeth.

"Well let's see what it costs you – because you will burn to nothing. We'll make sure of it." Nakiyah said, raising her arms.

"And so it begins." Samuel concluded.

* * *

The half-demons surrounded the six, circling them. They kept their eyes on Samuel's minions, ready to strike at any minute.

"Let's do this." Marina growled, her eyes glowing.

She raised her hands to the sky and drew lightning into her palms. The half demons formed fire in their hands and aimed them towards the coven. As they shot out the flames, Tiffany's eyes lit up purple. The scent of roses filled the air. The demons sniffed and moved towards her.

"I have a feeling this one will be a satisfying conquest." a man in a black suit said, licking his lips.

As he put his arms around Tiffany's waist and the other demons surrounded her, Marina aimed her hands towards the sky, lightning entering their bodies and frying them.

They burned into ashes as Nakiyah whipped up 120mph winds, blowing the ash into the atmosphere and sending six more slamming into building walls. Their bodies shattered into pieces, and Rayna shot blue and red waves of heat into them, burning them into nothing.

A few young half-demons surrounded Rose, grinning and growling, flames in their palms. Rose shook at first, but then she aimed her hands at the pavement beneath them. The asphalt shook with the frequency of a bubbling motion. The pavement opened up, and they sunk into boiling mud, screeches echoing from their dying forms.

Matthew and Nakiyah faced Samuel.

"So, I'm cursed with the two who hate each other," Samuel cackled, "This should be fun."

* * *

Nakiyah and Matthew sent their bursts of heat and energy into him, Matthew's red and blue, Nakiyah's white. Samuel shook a bit, his teeth chattering so hard they broke into pieces. Then he regained his stability and chuckled. His jagged teeth grew back.

"Fools." he cursed, "Matthew, have you forgotten how this started?"

"I'm not going to fall victim to your mind games." Matthew hissed, standing strong.

"Tituba forced me to sell my soul. I need you, Matthew, that's why I took your wife. I was weak and unable to fight without you." Samuel partially lied.

"...I don't believe you." Matthew challenged, backing up.

Samuel came up to his face, staring in his eyes.

"You know what you are, and you can't deny it. Your mission is the same as mine. If you kill them, this will end." Samuel chided, clutching his arm with a bony hand.

As Matthew looked at the flames in his red eyes, he felt a power enter him.

"Yes...you are one of us." Samuel beckoned.

As his hand clutched Matthew's wrist, power flowed into his veins. Matthew's eyes lit up red. Samuel smirked.

"Do it." he whispered.

"Matthew, no. He's trying to control you!" Rayna yelled in desperation.

Matthew turned to her, his eyes burning. He stepped towards her slowly, like an automaton. He raised his hands above his head, and a fireball formed.

"Matthew...please...remember us..." Rayna said, dropping to her knees.

A spark of blue entered his eyes as a coolness entered his heart. But his body was acting of its own accord. He could no longer control himself.

"Do it." he whispered, the fireball growing larger.

"I can't..." Rayna choked out, tears streaming down her cheeks.

"It's the only way." he stated, aiming his arms out straight.

Rayna gulped and murmured a mea culpa, before sending red and blue sparks into Matthew, his body convulsing and smoking. When the fireball was extinguished, she stopped, and he fell to the ground.

She rushed over to him and looked at the burns on his body.

"I couldn't kill you." she whispered.

"You tried. You did the right thing." he said, choking on the smoke coming from his body.

Rose rushed over.

"Dad..." she cried, tears trailing down her face.

"Fight. That's all you can do." Matthew ordered, touching her face.

Rose's eyes glowed amber as she headed towards a hoard of demons.

"Rayna, it's up to you and your aunt. End this." Matthew said, "I'll be okay."

Rayna's eyes glowed blue, sparking red. Nakiyah's eyes turned milky white. They faced Samuel, hands outstretched.

"Poor sap. You couldn't even kill him." Samuel laughed.

"I'll kill you – even if it means I die with you." Rayna growled.

Rayna shot her power into Samuel, squinting her eyes closed and putting every bit of her energy into it. Nakiyah swirled winds, making the energy circulate through his body. His skin began to burn but he clenched his teeth, raising his hands above his head.

"You...will...die..." he choked out, sending a fireball at them.

They dove out of the way. Rayna saw the fireball heading for *Midnight Tomes* – she shot a stream of her power at it and extinguished it.

"I will say...you're not dumb like SHE was." Samuel joked, smiling.

"Tituba wasn't dumb. She was right to get rid of the likes of you!" Nakiyah shouted.

As she shot her storm winds at him, attempting to slam him into a building, Rayna screamed "NO!" Samuel was a quick-shot, sending a fireball flying at her. Rayna sent a stream of her power at it, but it was too late. The fireball hit Nakiyah, burning her into nothing, her screams like nails on a chalkboard in the empty streets.

Rayna let out a blood-curdling screech, collapsing where Nakiyah had been standing, her hands touching the burn marks.

"One down...one to go." Samuel laughed.

* * *

Four half-demons headed towards Marina and Tiffany, a mix of men and women.

"Do your thing, babe." Marina said, looking at Tiffany.

Tiffany's eyes turned purple, and a scent of jasmine wafted through the air. The demons sniffed it and looked into her eyes, approaching her.

"Come here, my delicious lovelies." Tiffany crooned, swaying her hips.

As they came upon her, lightning struck them, sizzling them into nothing. Marina's eyes were silver, and she smiled.

Five demons came towards Rose.

"Your aunt is gone." one said, smiling.

"Your father and his girlfriend are next." another growled.

"And you are ours." the third one chuckled.

"You don't know who you're messing with." Rose hissed.

She wove her hands and petrified vines came up, entwining them together. They all struggled and tried to shoot flames at her, but the vines absorbed the power, scorching the demons. They screamed and struggled against them to no avail.

"Oh girls..." Rose called, smirking.

Tiffany and Marina stalked towards them, grinning. They aimed their hands at each other, creating purple and silver lightning, and shot it at the demons, frying them to bits of ember. Rose wove her hands again, the vines receding into the pavement.

"That was fun." she giggled.

As Rayna sent her red and blue power into Samuel, his strength fading, he chuckled.

"You strike in vain. You will die. So will he." he whispered.

Ash flew in the wind, and the flesh from his skull melted off half of it.

"You may melt me, but you will never destroy me." he insisted, sending a stream of fire against her power.

As the fire inched closer and closer to her, Rayna fell to her knees, her energy waning.

Marina, Tiffany, and Rose ran over. Rose sent the petrified vines around Samuel, tying him up. Marina and Tiffany were about to add their power, when they heard a voice say, "STOP!"

The flow of power stopped. At the sound of the voice, Samuel's fire died down to sparks.

Tituba.

Chapter Twenty-Three

Tituba's spirit form floated towards Samuel. She gazed into his eyes.

"What have you become?" she asked, "Is every drop of love burned out of you?"

"You bitch! You came back to watch me die – just like I saw my daughter die!" he screamed.

"No. I came to show you something." she replied.

Tituba raised her hand to his forehead. He tried to back away, but he was stuck. As her hand touched him, he closed his eyes.

Elizabeth looked out the window, anger flaring in her. What was her father doing with that woman?! She watched the sun to see when he would come home. As it began to set, it flickered – slow at first, then quickly, because of the leaves on the trees blowing in the wind. She began to convulse, falling on the floor. Samuel came in, holding her close and glaring at Tituba's shack.

"It was...epilepsy?" he asked, his jaw agape.

"Yes. I would never hurt your family – I told you I'd care for them." Tituba replied.

Samuel looked into her eyes, tears forming in his.

"I'm -" he began.

Suddenly, the pavement opened up, and the head demon rose from the ground.

"You're what?!" he demanded, "You sold half your soul! You don't feel a thing anymore!"

"I'm sorry." Samuel finished.

The vines went down. A glow of light surrounded Samuel, and he appeared as Tituba saw him in 1692.

"That's it. Your fate is sealed." the head demon sentenced.

As Samuel began to sink into the ground, he reached out for Tituba.

"Save me, beloved!" he pleaded.

She hesitated before grabbing his hand, trying to pull him out of the ground.

"Then you shall burn -" the head demon started to say.

Rayna, Rose, Marina, and Tiffany all aimed their hands at him, their eyes glowing. They sent their power into him, sending him sinking back into Hell.

"You shall never ever come back
Nor cause any pain
Your feet shall never in millions of years
Touch the earth again.
So mote it be."

"Damn you!!" he screamed as the pavement sealed back up, locking him below forever.

Tituba pulled Samuel out of the human sinkhole, and Rose closed it up.

"I'm your beloved?" she asked.

"You always have been," he said, caressing her cheek, "Your ancestors carried your presence to me all these centuries, resurrecting my love for you. But I was too blind with anger and hatred to let myself give in to it. Please forgive me." he said, getting down on one knee.

Tituba pulled him to a standing position.

"I forgive you." she said, taking his hands.

They kissed with passion, with love that centuries tore apart.

A beam of sun appeared from the sky.

"To Summerland?" she asked.

"With you? Forever." Samuel replied, entwining his fingers with her.

As they ascended the light staircase, Tituba paused. She looked at Matthew. She walked over to him, placing her hand on his heart and closing her eyes. The burns disappeared, and his pulse & heartbeat went back to normal. He opened his eyes, and his jaw went agape.

"You?" he asked.

"Yes, I returned to right things. I see you all did a good job, though." Tituba replied, her spirit form standing up.

"Keep the generations going." she instructed, smiling.

As Samuel and Tituba disappeared, they all looked at the burned spot where Nakiyah was last standing.

"Did Tituba know everything?" Matthew asked.

"She knew everything – once you die, it all becomes clear. She knew Samuel had no idea. It's like any crime of passion – they feel vilified in what they're doing. They don't all get forgiveness – Samuel was lucky." Rayna explained, tears falling down her face.

"That's a powerful love." Rose said, a tear slipping down her cheek.

"I hope you find someone who loves you that much one day." Matthew said to Rose, kissing her forehead.

"Let's get out of here. I'm exhausted." Tiffany said, yawning.

The five of them walked down the street – bonded for life.

Epilogue

Rose packed the last of her clothes into her suitcases and lined them up at the top of the stairs. Matthew walked up and looked at his daughter, smiling.

"Ready to be a famous artist?" he asked.

"Dad, it's gonna take years for me to get there. But college is a start." Rose replied.

"We're gonna miss you - " Matthew began.

"I'm coming home every day you know," Rose chuckled, hugging him, "You'll still see me. I'm just going to Salem State University."

"I know. It'll just be strange – you're your own woman now. You're not a little girl anymore." Matthew argued, hugging her tighter.

"Dad, it's starting to hurt." Rose said, pulling away.

Matthew released her.

"I gotta go finish dinner. I made your favorite – spaghetti with meatballs, hot sausage, and garlic bread." he said, grinning.

"I'll be right down!" Rose exclaimed, going into Rayna and Matthew's room.

Rayna sat on the teal toilet seat cover, staring at a white plastic stick. She and Matthew made love for six months, trying for another child. Matthew was back to grinding his teeth, and Rayna was on a diet to boost fertility. They tried everything except IVF because they didn't have the money for it.

Rose opened the door and stood there, arms crossed.

"Are you gonna tell me the results? Or am I gonna pace in front of the door all night?" Rose asked.

Rayna looked down and tears streamed down her cheeks. Rose took the stick and looked at it.

"A plus sign?" she asked, grinning.

"Yup." Rayna replied, smiling back.

"Does Dad know?" Rose asked.

"No, I want to surprise him. He didn't even know I took the test." Rayna whispered.

"When will you tell him?" Rose asked.

"When we go downstairs, but before we eat – I don't want him choking." Rayna said, laughing.

* * *

Rose and Rayna both galloped downstairs and into the kitchen.

"Two hungry witches," Matthew said, smirking, "What ever will I do?"

"Dish out the Italian food," Rayna said, pausing, "After all, I'm eating for two."

Matthew froze. He turned around slow like a figure in a music box. "We're..." he trailed off.

"Pregnant." Rayna said, smiling at the same time.

Matthew picked her up and swung her around. Rose's face glowed.

"Precious cargo!" Rayna warned.

Matthew guided her with caution to a chair and sat her down, putting the napkin on her lap, and serving everyone.

"I'm not a two year old." Rayna grumbled.

"Like you said, precious cargo." Matthew said, patting her head.

"You're gonna throw that back at me for nine months, aren't you?" Rayna asked.

"Yup." he replied, twirling his spaghetti, "Now eat."

"I have a feeling college will be a good experience," Rose said, biting into a slice of garlic bread, "It will be full of twists, turns, and, hopefully, love."

"NO more demons." Matthew said, raising an eyebrow.

"Well at least I know what to look for now." Rose argued.

Rayna chewed a meatball and cut up a sausage into small pieces.

"You're that hungry already?" Matthew asked, eyes widened.

"No, I need to keep my powers energized." Rayna said, patting his head.

"An eye for an eye, I suppose." he said, sipping his red wine.

"Dad, can I have a glass of wine?" Rose asked.

"Well...I suppose on your last night here, a little at home wouldn't hurt." Matthew begrudged.

He got up and got a juice glass and poured Rose enough to fill it.

"Dad, that's not even four ounces."

"It's enough for someone who's not 21." Matthew replied, narrowing his eyes at her.

"Fine." she huffed, sipping it.

As they ate, Rose stopped. She saw a forest, with paw prints in the snow. She heard a howl in her mind. Rose shivered.

"What's wrong?" Rayna asked, putting a hand on her shoulder.

"Nothing...just nerves over my algebra class." Rose brushed off.

"You'll do fine. Your dad is a whiz at math." Rayna insisted, squeezing the shoulder she was holding.

"Yeah, you've got the Master when you come home on weekends to help you." Matthew added, ruffling her hair.

Rose half-smiled.

Rayna ate her pasta with a vigorous energy, gulping down the orange juice Matthew had put in front of her. He refilled her glass two times during the meal, glad she was getting her vitamin C, but realizing shopping was in his future.

"I'm not going to have to buy out the supermarket am I?" he asked.

"Oh, just chocolate chunk cookies, potato chips, pickles, ice cream, lots of juice, plenty of bacon -" Rayna began

"Okay, okay...we will make a list tomorrow. We'll keep it posted on the refrigerator so I don't forget anything for nine months." Matthew cut her off, shaking his head as he swallowed some meatball pieces.

"I just want to be prepared for the cravings." Rayna argued

"Be prepared for the puking." Rose suggested.

"Oh Jesus. I forgot that part." Rayna groaned, holding her head.

"But we might get a baby girl out of it." Rose countered.

"OR a boy." Matthew emphasized.

"Women are stronger." Rose said

"How do you know that?" he asked.

"Rayna fried you a while back." she said with smugness.

"Thanks for reminding me I almost died."

Matthew cleared their plates and piled them in the sink. He reached into the oven and pulled out an apple pie. He drizzled caramel sauce on each piece and topped them with whipped cream, meanwhile pouring three cups of coffee and putting a container of pumpkin pie spice creamer on the table.

"Geez, you're gonna make me blow up like a balloon." Rayna complained.

"You'll be wanting this kind of meal every night in a few months." Matthew said, kissing her cheek.

"Fine. I'll eat it." Rayna replied, smirking.

"Yeah, that's what I thought – I know my women love my baking skills." Matthew retorted, winking.

As they ate dessert, dreams of the future hung in the air, now that a new generation was on the way. Girl or boy, it would be well loved – and powerful.

* * *

That night, as they slept, Rayna tossed and turned. She kept seeing Nakiyah burning away. She screamed as the fireball hit her. Matthew heard her and shook her, waking her up.

"Babe, it's okay." He insisted, rubbing her back.

"I can't get it out of my dreams." Rayna choked out, crying.

"Look, when we go drop Rose at college tomorrow, you'll forget all about it." Matthew said, kissing her forehead.

"She'll be unprotected. What are we gonna do?" Rayna asked.

"We're gonna let her live her life. She's an adult now, and she's strong."

"I worry all the time." Rayna argued.

"Samuel is reformed and with Tituba. We consecrated the ground with that spell – the other demon can't come back. Samuel's group was destroyed. Do I need to go on?" He asked.

"I miss her." Rayna whispered.

"I know you do, babe, but she's always with you. You know that."

"I know." Rayna said, laying down and clutching her childhood bunny to her chest.

Matthew spooned her, kissing the back of her neck.

"It'll all be okay. I promise." he said, pulling her close.

As they closed their eyes, the light from the full moon shone in the window.

And a howl echoed in the wind outside.

Acknowledgments

To my mom – for reading every single page of my book as I wrote it and helping me make revisions along the way and being my first beta reader, as a fan of romance novels – for supporting me emotionally and mentally through the whole process. I love you.

To Eric – for being my unofficial editor, reading every scene and giving me constructive criticism on everything – for believing in this book from the initial idea and in me – for calming me down when the editing and business end of the publishing process triggered my anxiety. I love you eternally.

To Mr. and Mrs. Nierstedt for getting me the Black Sabbath compilation for Christmas that fueled many of the pages in this book – it was my driving force through the harder times when I felt like I couldn't write.

To the memory of Tituba and the victims of the Salem Witch Trials – you are forever in my memory, from when I visited Salem as a teenager to now. I altered history and facts to create a work of fiction, but I am hoping it changes how people perceive and think of things – and captures their hearts and minds.

And to Disney, Bette Midler, Sarah Jessica Parker, and Kathy Najimy – watching "Hocus Pocus" during the end of summer of 2018 was the impetus for this book. If it wasn't for that movie, I never would've researched the Salem Witch Trials – and this novel never would have been born.

About the Author

Kristin Bapst has a Bachelor's Degree in English from Kean University. She has been writing since she was young – getting her poetry published in her college years in Kean University's literary magazine, *Creation Space*. She also had a poem, "My Father's Marlboros", published in an online literary journal. She loves Marvel movies, Disney animated movies, 90's nostalgia, the Golden Girls, reading, music, the ocean, and her dog. She currently lives in New Jersey.

https://twitter.com/dreamer984
https://www.facebook.com/KBAuthor919/
https://kristinbapstauthor.com[1]

---

1. https://kristinbapstauthor.com/

Printed by Amazon Italia Logistica S.r.l.
Torrazza Piemonte (TO), Italy

15107397R00116